PECU*LIAR* FABRICATIONS

SHORT FICTIONS AND FAKE-NEWS

CHRISTMAS LETTERS

(PLUS A FEW OTHER TREATS TOSSED IN WHEN YOU WEREN'T LOOKING)

PECULIAR FABRICATIONS

SHORT FICTIONS AND FAKE-NEWS

CHRISTMAS LETTERS

(PLUS A FEW OTHER
TREATS TOSSED IN WHEN
YOU WEREN'T LOOKING)

JEFFERY VILES

BEAVER'S POND PRESS
MINNEAPOLIS, MN

Edited by Wendy Weckwerth

ISBN: 978-1-64343-899-3
Library of Congress Catalog Number: 2020903402
Printed in Canada
First Printing: 2020
24 23 22 21 20   5 4 3 2 1

 Beaver's Pond Press, Inc.
939 Seventh Street West
Saint Paul, MN

(952) 829-8818
www.BeaversPondPress.com

To order, visit www.ItascaBooks.com or call
1-800-901-3480 ext. 118. Reseller discounts available.

For Savannah, Cooper, and, especially, Rebekah.
You make my golden years golden.

ALSO BY JEFFERY VILES

The Sasquatch Murder
(A Love Story)

Finalist, 2017 Indie Book of the Year (Clarion/Foreword)
Finalist, 2018 Best Book Award (American Book Fest)

www.sasquatchmurder.com

"A genre-bending romp"

"A remarkable story . . . The writing is precise and flawless
. . . The dialogue from his diverse characters had me
laughing out loud . . . *The Sasquatch Murder* rocks!"

—Readers' Favorite

"No typical Bigfoot tale . . . *The Sasquatch Murder* is an
accomplished and thoroughly enjoyable tale, the kind of
book one is sorry to finish because it's such good company."

—Clarion/Foreword Reviews

"Viles writes in a crisp, balanced prose that's laden with
wonderful details . . . An earnest, thoughtful story about
an unplanned discovery."

—Kirkus

CONTENTS

A NOTE FROM THE AUTHOR:
About the Fake-News Christmas Letters

We've all seen them, those newsy letters from friends often tucked inside a Christmas card. They recount the family's events, travels, and successes in the past year. And bully for them. It's nice to be brought up to date on the lives and triumphs of friends.

But I couldn't help wondering how far you could go if you weren't constrained by facts. If you could just make it all up and have some fun. So I did.

Herewith, then, are the four annual Christmas letters I sent out to friends for their amusement, escalating the ridiculous and phony achievements each year until Fake-News Christmas Letter #4, when things went south. I think they liked that one best. The letters are staggered among the short fictions, and I hope they amuse you. No offense whatsoever is intended to those who send out real Christmas letters. Keep them coming.

JOE AND GORGEOUS GEORGE

FEMALE 911 DISPATCHER: 911. What is the nature and address of your emergency?

CALLER: Who is this?

DISPATCHER: This is the 911 emergency line. What is your call-back number?

CALLER: Uh. I need an ambulance.

DISPATCHER: OK. Tell me exactly what happened, and give me your call-back number.

CALLER: Uh. This is Joe. I'm Joe.

DISPATCHER: OK, Joe. Where do you need the ambulance?

JOE: I'm in this phone booth. I didn't know they had phone booths anymore.

DISPATCHER: All right. What's the address there?

JOE: Address? I don't know. Wait a minute.

(*Twenty-second pause.*)

DISPATCHER: OK, sir. Did you dial 911?

JOE: Yeah, right. That's it. I called *911*.

DISPATCHER: Joe, I need a location if you want an ambulance. What street are you on?

JOE: Uh. Yeah. I do. 'Cause I'm bleeding. Uh, I'm in this phone booth outside the Stop-and-Go. That's it. I'm at this Stop-and-Go way out on . . . wait a minute, what's the name of the street? Huffston or something—at the Stop-and-Go.

DISPATCHER: What's the nearest side street?

JOE: Hold on. (*Fifteen-second pause.*) Yo!

DISPATCHER: Yes, Joe?

JOE: Now let me see. Carlson? Carlton?

DISPATCHER: Carsman?

JOE: There you go. There you go.

DISPATCHER: OK. And you need an ambulance?

JOE: That's where I'm at. In the phone booth. Now first let me tell you what happened. I'm going down the road minding my own bidness and a crazy-ass deer jumped out and ran his antlers straight into the side of my car.

DISPATCHER: Sir. Just a second. Are you injured?

JOE: Now wait a minute. Let me tell you. I get out and pick up the deer and it's heavy, see, and it's sprawled out there and looks dead. I try to get him in the trunk of my car but the deer won't fit so I lay him in the back seat. I'm driving down the road again minding my own bidness again, and this crazy deer woke up and bit me on the back of my neck. He bit me and he kicked hell out of my car. And now I'm in the phone booth. The deer bit me in the neck and I stop and get out and a big yellow dog runs up and sees the deer trying to get out my car and the dog starts barking and bites me on the leg. Well, I hit the dog with my tire iron I was using to try and get the deer out. So I got a hurt leg and a hurt neck and the dog won't let me out the phone booth. He keeps barking at me and the deer. He wants the deer. Now who gets the deer, me or the dog?

DISPATCHER: Sir, are you injured? Do you want the ambulance?

JOE: Injured? Lady, I'm bit in the neck and the leg—hold on—the damn dog—hold on. The dog is getting in the phone booth and trying to bite me again. Hey! Get out of here. Hey! Stop it! Hold on. Get out of here!

DISPATCHER: Sir? Do you want the ambulance?

JOE: Hey, there they go. Look at that. The crazy deer kicked his way out of my car and took off toward the woods. The dog is chasing him. I'll be damned. Look at 'em go. Yo. Hey, lady, just forget the ambulance. I'm getting my sorry, bleeding butt down the road. Look at that back seat!

(*Click.*)

DISPATCHER: Sir? Sir?

(*Click.*)

The 911 operator leans back in her chair, laughing and shaking her head, as Joe revs an older Chevy the color of mud with a dented door and ripped-up back seat. Joe starts to drive away, then considers his wounds and circles the parking lot. He limps into the Stop-and-Go bathroom.

Joe mutters profanely as he looks at himself in the mirror. "Wish my ex-wife could see me now." He tries but fails to suppress a belch that rivals an elephant's rumble, the gassy leftover from three Bud Lights after work at the Five O'Clock Somewhere Bar and Grill. The mirror displays an unremarkable man with a crooked nose and skin the color of latte. Six feet two and thirty pounds overweight at age forty-four, Joe's curly dark hair is moving out and middle-age spread is moving in. The deer nip on his neck is bright red and surrounded by a halo of stress rash. The dog bite on his leg is worse. The concept of rabies is crackling dimly through his synapses. His neck and leg sting as he washes them with cheap soap.

Joe buys a sixteen-ounce Miller High Life and a PayDay as he strolls back to his damaged car. He drives away, craning his neck toward the woods where the deer and dog vanished. Half a mile through the evening twilight, he's flashed by the lights of an oncoming car, which reminds him to turn on his own headlights. Just then he catches an unsavory whiff of the gamey deer scat in his back seat. He mumbles a protest, pulls to the side of the road, gets out to pop the trunk lid, and then peers into the random mess. He extracts a set of jumper cables so old they could pass for an archeological discovery and is pleased to find that the clamps still work. He uses them like kitchen tongs to daintily remove the deer droppings, then lights a peeling Rum Crook cigar from the glove compartment and blows a cloud of smoke toward the back seat and floorboard as an air freshener.

Joe is closing the doors for departure when he notices a neon-ringed sign pulsing in front of a large tent across the road. *Gorgeous George for Jesus,* the sign flashes. A few cars are parked by the tent, and Joe decides to visit. His curiosity outweighs his desire to get home. He blows more cigar smoke toward the back and cracks the rear windows before walking to the tent entrance. He drains the last of the High Life and discards the can in a trash barrel.

Twenty-two men and women fill the front few rows of one hundred fifty folding chairs inside the muggy tent. Joe sits down away from the others, closes his eyes in the warmth, and wipes away the half tear that squeezes out. At first from a distance and then as if she were sitting next to him, Joe hears, or imagines he hears, the voice of Leena, his ex-wife. She is saying it all again: *The truth? You think you're ready for the truth, you low-life bastard! OK, fine. Here's some truth for you. You're not even Charles Joseph's real father. I was knocked up when I met you. After the wedding it was easy to say he was yours. How's that for some truth, Mister Screwed-My-Sister?*

Nine years have passed, but the night Leena told him the truth seems like ten minutes ago to Joe. Sitting quietly in the warm tent he not only recalls her words, but can still feel their sting, like a slap to the face or a 12-gauge to the gut. He knew instantly she wasn't lying. The revelation might have sent Joe into a blind rage but didn't. He remembers clearly the thirty seconds of paralysis before he walked wordlessly into their apartment's closet, packed his things, and left without speaking. In fact, Joe didn't speak directly to Leena ever again. The divorce was quick. The ensuing years passed in a blur. Even Calera, his fifth girlfriend in those nine years and the only one to make Joe consider marriage again, doesn't know the details of him and Leena and the young boy Charlie. A loud voice at the front of the tent causes Joe to shift in his chair and pay attention to the preacher for a moment.

"GOD DON'T NEED THINKERS, HE NEEDS B'LEEVERS IN THIS GREAT LAND," shouts Gorgeous George into his microphone as he storms across the draped stage. "Get on your feet and sing 'Battle Hymn of the Republic' with me."

George holds his Bible high and the twenty-two jump to their feet. Joe sits. The faithful sing with gusto but little talent. An excitable small man with thinning red hair and a glued-on smile hammers chords on an upright piano.

George is no longer gorgeous. His days as a professional wrestler with curly blonde hair and a V-shaped torso are many years gone. An extra fifty pounds have made the *V* into an *O*. His shaggy eyebrows and basset-hound jowls give George a drooped demeanor, but the expression yields to his piercing hawk's eyes and booming voice.

"America has hit the skids," he bellows as the song fades away. "People of God, you are the only ones who can save her." Behind George is a bright red lightbulb that blinks every two seconds above a hand-stenciled sign in black and yellow that declares: "Every time this light blinks another human soul plunges into the torment of hell!"

The hour-long sermon of George Garrison Grimes is beyond hellfire and damnation, beyond warning of fiery flames licking at the toes of mortal man. It's a masterpiece of rightwingedness tailored as perfectly to his audience as red wine to lamb chops.

"AMEN!" shout the twenty-two in unison as George drips sweat and calls for the government to put a stop to the drug epidemic. The sound startles a drowsy Joe. He opens his eyes wide, tilts his head back, and takes a deep breath.

"And another thing," George growls, pointing a crooked finger at the front row. "Every one of them Socialists in Hollywood and every mother's son of an MTV rock singer is sticking a knife in America's belly with their godless trash. This has got to stop, my friends. We got to arm ourselves if we want to be right-thinking, Christian people. Arm ourselves with Bible ideas and blue steel at the same time. This is the only way us children of God can STOP the abortions, STOP the foulness in our televisions and movies, STOP the mind-sucking drugs and casual sex and damnable demons of pornography, and STOP the scum that walk our streets with a hand out for money they'll spend on booze." He stops to catch his breath before continuing with arms outstretched to conduct. "My fellow believers, stand up with me now and sing to the top of your lungs." George launches the singing with "Onward, Christian Soldiers, marching as to war" in a booming *basso profundo* that shakes the tent and fortifies the convictions of every man, woman, and child in earshot. Except for Joe, that is. Joe is now in a doorknob-dead sleep. His large head is tilted sideways and the angry-looking red neck from the deer bite makes him look like he might have just been hauled down from the gallows.

"Thank you, brothers and sisters," says George in a suddenly humble voice as the song ends and the collection basket is passed. "Give till it hurts. This ministry is expensive to operate." When the basket has made its rounds George says, "Now come to the back and shake my hand."

He moves to a long table near the tent's entrance and begins a brisk sale of sermon tapes, Old Glory belt buckles the size of cell phones, prophecy pamphlets, and a bound-in-faux-leather volume costing $39.95 titled

Seven Bible Reasons Why Elvis Presley Did Not Go to Hell. As George makes change and shakes hands he wipes sweat from his face with a red bandana. His tongue darts back and forth across his lips like a bullfrog. Behind George is a large easel bearing a framed poster of a New York City wrestling card from long ago, proudly showing George in his tight trunks with his long blonde hair flowing behind. He was clearly a mass of hard muscle.

When the last of the flock has departed, the piano player helps count the money. He is Kirkpatrick McGonigle, a native of Galway and George's right hand since the wrestling days. He hasn't softened his Irish brogue despite decades wandering America. He's George's employee, but McGonigle is no lickspittle. "What about that one over there?" he says, nodding toward napping Joe. "The lad may have had a wee drop or two. Possibly was spitting cotton and needed adult beverages."

"Tough customer," says George. "I tried to yell him awake during the sermon but no luck." McGonigle and George both stare at Joe like he's a biology specimen. "Shoot," George says. "I wouldn't say no to a wee drop myself. And I know you wouldn't. The last time an Irishman turned down a nip of John Barleycorn the Vikings were marching around the Ring of Kerry. Let's see if we can take our sleepy buddy with us. I'm tired of listening to your blarney—and, besides, I'll get a donation out of him."

"Oh, will you now? I'll be seriously doubting there's any blood in that turnip," says McGonigle.

A hint of a smile crosses George's face. "All these years and you still haven't learned, have you my little Mick? Looks like a wager is at hand. Shall we say twenty bucks?"

"Make it thirty, but he's got to give at least ten. Anything less, you lose."

"Done," says George. "Wake the man up, and here we go."

McGonigle touches Joe on the shoulder while the sleeping man is channeling the deer coming back to life. He grunts and jumps to his feet, knocking over two chairs. "Hoowah," Joe growls.

"Hey, hey, buddy, take it easy, take it easy," says McGonigle, backing away. "Easy, my boy. You fell asleep."

"Lordy. I'm sorry there, guy," Joe says. "Didn't mean to doze off. I was having a bad dream. Sorry. It's been a rough night and I drank some beer and I usually don't drink much."

"No problem at all, brother," George interrupts, putting a beefy arm around Joe. "Come on back to our trailer, and let's all settle our nerves. The world's going to end, but it won't be tonight."

"Well, thank you there, preacher," Joe says, not wanting to insult the man any further after sleeping through his sermon. "I can't stay long, but thank you."

* * *

The trailer isn't a trailer but a retired Greyhound bus with *Gorgeous George for Jesus* stenciled down both sides. It's been converted to a rolling bed and breakfast, complete with ice maker and big-screen TV. McGonigle pours three fingers of Old Charter for each of them and they sit on floor-mounted wing chairs with fold-out tray tables.

"Hey, don't worry so much about falling asleep," George says in response to Joe's apologies. "You're not the first, and you won't be the last. The way you shot awake and said you were having a bad dream sounds like you might be having some troubles, my friend. Anything I could do to help? That's what our ministry's all about, you see, and even though it takes every nickel to keep it going, that's what we do."

"No. It ain't anything new," Joe responds. "I just had a nightmare 'cause I got a damn nightmare of an ex-wife, that's all. Pardon my French, preacher."

"Not a problem," says George. "Well, well, woman troubles. Me and the Irishman here can tell you some stories. Can't we, Mick? Tell our friend about your little woman."

"I lost her to Colonel Sanders and Burger King," says McGonigle. "A common tale it is not, but fast food took her away. I'm down in the islands, see, and I strike it up with this little cocoa beauty. She's about ninety pounds, tops. Well, I bring her home to Baltimore, and we set up house. George and I were split up for a while about then, so I commence to selling encyclopedias. Pretty good at it too. It paid the bills, and she had a part-time job. But every time I leave the house here she goes to get fried chicken or Whopper burgers, sometimes both. Little thing could eat like a sumo wrestler, she could, and it wasn't long before she's looking like one too. George thinks I'm prone to exaggerate a bit, but that little thing was weighing a good two hundred thirty or two hundred forty pounds when I packed her up and sent her back to the Dominican Republic, as I surely did. The food was just too easy for the taking here. To this day I feel bad that it happened, and I hope she's OK back at home. One of these days I need to get down there to see how she's doing."

"And my own story is no better," says George. "Kirkpatrick and I share some of the blame, to be sure, but we've not been lucky with women. I was nineteen—a hundred and ninety pounds of farm-built muscle—when the carnival came to town. My folks had acreage where we lived in Arkansas. The carnival had a wrestler, and if you could stay in the ring with him for three minutes after you paid him two bucks, he'd give you back twenty. I watched three grown men try and fail before I climbed in and handed him my last two dollars. He knew too many slick moves for me to beat him, of course, but I did stay in it for three minutes to take the twenty. He told the crowd I was strong as a mule. He was so proud of me he took me along on the road. Thurman Eagle Wing was the name he went by. Supposed to be Indian, but I don't think he was. Just some big, strong guy from Oklahoma who taught me all the wrestling moves."

"I thought we were talking about women," McGonigle says.

George gives him a stern look. "I'll get to that. Our friend here could take comfort from other tales of women woes—right, friend?"

"Joe," says Joe as he sips the bourbon. "Call me Joe."

"Sure thing, Joe. Just relax and take it easy. You're among the Lord's servants here, and we're all looking for inner peace in one way or another, aren't we? Well, where was I? Oh, yeah. So Thurman and I constituted a wrestling team with the carnival. We'd spell each other, and we did OK continuing with the three-minute game. But this is before there got to be big money in wrestling. Long before I took the calling and was born again. I had blonde hair and let it grow long, down past my shoulders. The customers liked it. 'Hey, pretty boy,' they'd call me. 'Look at Gorgeous up there.'

"Well, there were a few girls along the way who liked long hair too. I'll admit it. I was a sinner and a heathen. I really got the bug for one down in south Alabama. She was as pretty as they come. I jumped ship on Thurman and the carnival. Didn't really care for all the traveling. He wished me good luck. I got a steady job driving a bread-truck route and seeing my gal every evening. That was a good couple of months. And then she wanted to get married. I was twenty by then, and she'd told me she was twenty-two years old. But we weren't married a week before I found out she was thirty-two and had been married twice before. I could've gotten used to that, but as soon as we were married she changed for the worse. Got hard and bossy. Made me cut my hair, first thing, and nothing I did would suit her. Something kept her from being like she was before, when we were dating. There were about two days a month when she was good company. I lasted about six months before I was gone and she finally signed the divorce papers two years later. Things worked out pretty good for me, though. I went back to wrestling and became Gorgeous George and got about half famous doing it. Made good money and spent it all. As I look back on it now, I see that all the fakery and bamboozling was nothing but Satan's work."

George leans back, studies his fingernails and says: "Joe, let me say once again you're among friends here. Tell us your woman story and leave your burden."

Joe sips the last of his bourbon. He tilts his head back, purses his lips, and says: "I don't know. It don't get talked about much. I probably need to get going."

"Now, no need to rush," says George. "Unload your troubles to me, Christian friend. I'm here to help, and I've got experience. Maybe I can be of service."

"OK, OK," says Joe. "You got me. You boys think you've been through some hard spots, and it sounds like you have. But let me tell you about Miss Leena. I'm pretty sure there's never been anything sorrier than she turned out.

"First time I seen her, she was prancing a line dance in a cowboy bar. I give her a little wave and she smiles back. We had some drinks, and one thing led to another, so she goes home with me. I was driving a concrete truck for Brainert's Cement and she started riding the truck with me. I was sure glad for the company. The next thing you know, I'm married to her. We got married inside of two weeks. Nine months later Charlie Joe is born, and you never seen a prouder daddy than me.

"I took a second job driving a street sweeper at night. We were doing OK, but it seemed like Leena was drinking more and more. I'm no teetotaler myself, never have been, but this woman was parched. Drank vodka in the morning and beer at night. I'm working the two jobs and paying the bills so I didn't see her all that much, even though she quit her job to take care of Charlie Joe. When I'd get home late at night and she'd been drinking, we'd fight like alley cats, mostly about money. We'd try not to wake the baby, but that didn't always work. I was sick of working two jobs just so she could drink. When she got to leaving the baby at her sister's so she could hit the bars, I got to talking with her sister quite a bit. I'd get to our apartment late and no Leena or Charlie Joe so, you know, I'd head on over to her sister's to get the boy. Now, her sister was a divorced woman, a good-looking woman, and we'd talk some and the next thing you know that hug at the door had led to something else. I suppose we shouldn't have done it, but I kinda felt like Leena drove me to it."

George breaks in, "And who could disagree with that? You were working your fingers to the bone for someone who didn't even—"

"Now wait," says Joe. "Let me tell the whole thing while I'm telling. So Leena finds out from her sister what was happening and that kicks off the biggest argument you ever saw or heard, and I'm not kidding. No use talking about all the things that was said, but in the end she finished the argument by telling me the God's hard truth. She told me I was not the father of Charlie Joe. She'd known all along and just used me like a plow horse. Five years working like a dog for nothing. It was mean as a thing can be. I went all dead inside when she told me. She said I was worse because I'd been screwing her sister. There was nothing left to say. I knew somehow it was the truth, so I just walked out and never spoke to her again. Or talked about it until tonight."

"Joe, you are now in the 'Relationship Woes Hall of Fame' in my way of thinking," says George. "Your experience makes the ones Kirkpatrick and I suffered seem like spit in a monsoon. And now that we've all let our hair down a bit, I hope some of that weight has been lifted from your shoulders. I'd like to ask you to join our church tonight and be included in our future prayers. For a simple small donation we put your name in our prayer book and all our members across this wonderful country pray for each other from the book. You're never going to have to think of that woman again with all the prayer power behind you. Here, let me show you what the book looks like."

Joe shoots a look at McGonigle and catches the smirk he can't hide. The Irishman tries to look away, but it's too late. Joe looks back at George. His expression is sincere but a twinkle in his eyes raises suspicion. Joe jumps to his feet. "Hey, never mind. I'm late. I need to leave." His face is hot and his hands are shaking.

George blocks the way out with his big arms outstretched and says, "Hold on, good friend. Let me talk to you for just a few seconds."

George turns his back to find the prayer book and is startled when Joe tries to shove him out of the way, barking, "I said never mind."

Joe grabs George by the shoulders to twist him to the right, but George's instinct is swift and effective. He swings his right leg close to his left and then quickly behind Joe's legs. Simultaneously he elbows Joe's chest and throws his weight against the elbow. Joe is flung backwards, trips over George's leg, and staggers into the coffee table, sending the bourbon glasses flying.

McGonigle is doubled over trying to hold back the half wheeze, half laugh filling his lungs.

Joe lets out an *oof* and is immediately held tightly in a headlock before he can recover. "Get him out of here," George says calmly but firmly. "Get this dude out of here." George releases Joe at the door of the bus and gives him a polite shove outside.

Joe's sore, deer-bitten red neck is throbbing from the headlock, and when he shinned the coffee table, he hit the exact spot the dog bit. He walks away.

McGonigle follows. "Hey, Joe. I'm sorry we upset you. You're a fine fellow in my book, you are. Don't let George get you down. He's always working the crowd, you know what I mean?"

"Not really. I just know I've had a rough evening, and then he got me talking just to put the pinch on. It was too much. I lost my temper. Something got into me."

"Well, don't worry yourself. He didn't mean a thing by it," McGonigle assures him. "By the way. Whatever happened to the boy you thought you fathered."

Joe opens his car door and checks for odors. The sweet smell of the Rum Crook cigar.

He turns to look McGonigle in the eye. "This has been one hell of an evening. You don't even know about the deer and the dog. But I'll be glad to tell you about Charlie Joe. He's just about to turn fifteen and making straight As in school. He's whip smart and wants to be an architect. No doubt in my mind that's what he'll be. He's doing fine, just fine. He's lived with me for eight years now and says I'm his father no matter what because I'm the one who loves him and takes care of him. He saw through Leena within a year of my leaving, even though he was a little guy. Told her he wanted to live with me. I was all for it. We get along great and if I hurry home he'll still be up. He's gonna get quite a kick out of my story about this crazy day."

Joe gives McGonigle a quick wave and guns his aging car away from the tent revival onto the wide street. He is driving a little too fast and his reactions are a little bit slow, courtesy of the beer and whiskey. He's thinking about Charlie Joe and looking at his Timex when a doe and her fawn cross the road in front of him. He hits the brakes hard, but not quick enough.

FEMALE DISPATCHER: 911. What is the nature and address of your emergency?

JOE: Hey, it's me again.

FAKE-NEWS CHRISTMAS LETTER #1

Dear Friends,

We're especially pleased with what our family has accomplished this year, and we'd like to share our thoughts with you during this Christmas season.

Our workload and the resultant stress were interfering with our afternoon naps, so we decided to take action. Both Jeff and his significant other, Rebekah, decided early in the year to leave their jobs so they could be stay-at-home child raisers for wonderful little Savannah. Jeff's early investment in Apple made this possible. Now each day is like a holiday.

In the spring we began faithful daily workouts and changes in diet to eliminate fat and sugar. We've never felt stronger or healthier. Jeff runs five miles each morning and Rebekah works out for an hour on our home gym's elliptical treadmill. In the afternoons we take ten-mile bike rides with Savannah in her little pull cart, and we pick up all the trash and recycling along rural roads and trails. Jeff's total body fat is down to 1.8 percent, and Rebekah's is about the same.

In the evenings we cook together, allowing ourselves a healthy six ounces of fine Bordeaux each. Highlights of recent family meals include miso-poached salmon with celery-root puree; grilled ahi tuna in phyllo baskets with a lime, ginger, and cilantro marinade; steamed Dover sole with lemon verbena and asparagus tips in black truffle oil; and applewood-smoked free-range chicken (skin removed, of course) with tomatillo relish and local watercress we gathered while biking. It's a joy to work with the earth's precious bounty.

Savannah has shown remarkable intellectual proclivities for an infant. Her English is crisp and clear, so we've found her a private tutor for Spanish and French. Her tutor, Niko, also speaks her native Japanese to Savvy, and our little princess can already write and pronounce all the Japanese alphabet symbols.

Jeff's older son, Gabriel, completed his studies at M.I.T. and joined the Peace Corps. His initial posting is Rwanda, where his engineering degree allows him to help the Rwandans successfully dig wells to irrigate their crops. Our sense of pride at his selflessness is profound.

Rebekah and Jeff continue their letter-writing campaign on behalf of political prisoners worldwide. They make it a point to write to state and federal solons at least once a month. Rebekah continues her volunteer work at the hospital and Red Cross, of course, while Jeff is now a Big Brother to an even dozen underprivileged children. And he still doesn't mind the calls in the middle of the night as a volunteer fireman, unless he's given blood that day. Rebekah's Sunday school classes are still winning awards, and she's proud when Jeff fills in as a visiting preacher for small, rural churches.

We certainly don't want to suggest that our way is the only way, but we can honestly report that eliminating guilt, stress, fat, sugar, and selfishness have provided our most joyous holiday season ever.

MERRY CHRISTMAS!

VIỆT NAM

Behold, comrades:
> 2.7 million homegrown killers.
> Temporarily insane by training and law, but less
> than 10 percent of our generation.

You will forgive us now, you croc-smile people.
> Our faces are washed, and we are clean.
> This is how it was.

Snakes, green and shiver deadly.
> Palm trees, rice paddies, gnawing bugs—green.
> Helicopters, green, like angry aging parrots.

But why were the body bags green?
> The green of betel nut–stained teeth.
> Who decided that?

What Pentagon committee gravely pondered green,
> Or camouflage, and never, ever considered the
> Bags could be blood red, or black, or why not white?

Like the angels who would have to ride all
Broken up and trussed inside?

Skin and hair took chafe from thermal heat
And phobic mist unknown before and vented bile
In volcanic welts, or sores, that wouldn't heal
Unless, *and if,* you reached home shores.

Always, too, the smells were wrong. Not air, not grass,
Not even dirt. But pungent napalm, diesel-burning
Fecal urns, oily steel and decomposing wastage
Mounded heedlessly afield.

America the beautiful, with amber waves and crooked
Smiles and glad-you're-homes and charming lies
And unwashed, hairy dropouts who claim to know
What's right
(And wrong).

And time,
The one great savior of us all, to almost
Irrigate away that stale dark night.

DAY OF THE BUTTERFLIES

The bright morning sun insisted on a clear and warm awakening. The soft rain shower during the night was forgotten. The salty Caribbean breeze smelled so good that Fidel Lenin Medina wanted to catch it in a glass and drink it.

Moving air was persistent but only strong enough to make the palm fronds gently dance. Lenny, as he was known (because he'd never shared his father's revolutionary fervor), stood in the unadorned doorway of his two-room house and filled his lungs with the invigorating air again and again. He started his days this way and thought of the habit as his oxygen bath. He felt physically and mentally improved by the embrace of sun and fresh air. As he'd done each Monday since the tragic and mysterious death of his wife eight months earlier, Lenny wore only his loose underwear as he hung his three white shirts to dry on the small lemon tree by the front door.

Had a neighbor or passerby noticed his half-naked appearance, nothing would have been thought of it. The rural, seaside village had always been casual to the extreme, even accepting complete nudity at the beach along the Rio Tortuga, which disappeared into the estuary nearby. A few nudist tourists even showed up around Christmas each year. Lenny went back inside the small house, sat down with a cup of strong chocolate, and looked out a crooked window down the village road. He hadn't prayed that morning, so he dropped to one knee beside the breakfast chair and asked God to take Nedra into his kingdom and to let him understand.

The neighbor nicknamed Gatekeeper was removing his handmade wooden barrier from the village road. Lenny watched. For several years Gatekeeper had been able to collect a small toll since a surveyor's error caused the road to cross his property without permission. This practice was no longer tolerated by the regional militia. His opening and closing of the gate each morning and night were ceremonial. As Lenny watched Gatekeeper unblock the dirt road, he saw the old man suddenly stop, transfixed, and stare at something in the distance. In a moment Lenny could make out what Gatekeeper already saw, an immense cloud of silver butterflies approaching.

The view was astonishing. An uncountable number of the butterflies danced on the light wind and darted in random directions to escape the predatory birds that dipped and dived into the cloud. Lenny abandoned his breakfast and walked outside again as the first of the butterflies swept past. Their silver, bow-tie wings and dark undersides created waves of alternating colors in the sky.

The creatures seemed to be aligning their movement to the village road.

He laughed. It was the first genuine laugh, spontaneous and without overcast, to animate him since Nedra had mysteriously drowned.

"*Hola*, Gatekeeper. What do you make of this?" Lenny shouted at the old man now nearly hidden by the layers of two- and three-inch butterflies.

"*Dios mío!*" he shouted back. "What can this be? Where do they come from? It must be a sign from heaven."

"If we want it to be, then it is," Lenny called. "They are beautiful. What is God telling us?"

"That he still loves us despite our behavior, I would think. Though who is to say? *Muy magnifico!*"

Lenny smiled at his neighbor's interpretation. "*Comprendo*," he said, then muttered to himself: "Why are we always so superstitious? It is a simple migration."

Gatekeeper moved to the side of the road and sat on an overturned bucket. Lenny stood quietly in his doorway, watching the butterflies and adjusting his underwear to a more modest position. The silver cloud moved in rhythm with the breeze by swirling one moment in a thick mass and the next in a thin stream. There was no ebb in the passing flow. Lenny walked outside to the road and tried to plunge his hand into the cloud to catch one from the air. No success. He went back inside and dressed.

At the table he dipped a dry biscuit into the chocolate and chewed it vigorously. His prominent features and broad nose were outlined sharply in the light that shafted through the window. Lenny watched the silvery shimmer from the butterflies and thought of snow, though he'd never seen it in person. He was fascinated by subtitled television programs that showed places like Chicago covered in snow. A sudden childish squeal and the sound of splashing water reminded him the morning ritual had begun. His wife's final gift, the surprise daughter born fewer than three months before her death, was receiving her bath. Laureano loved the water. She splashed with her hands and feet and giggled at the mess she created.

"Remedios," Lenny called to the young woman who lived in his house and cared for Laureano, "which of you is getting wetter?"

"Me, for sure," Remedios responded. "I don't need a bath after a morning with this little dolphin."

Lenny leaned back in his rickety wooden chair and listened with his eyes closed. Laureano was pure treasure, a beautiful but unexpected child. Nedra had been forty-three; Lenny, forty-four. They had two grown children living in Santo Domingo. He couldn't look at his daughter without thinking of Nedra and feeling a wave of helplessness. The baby's arrival had been awkward considering their age and Nedra's disposition at the time. She mistook the early feelings of pregnancy for the beginning of her change of life, a development she welcomed. Older women in the village told Nedra when the change was complete, the best days of her life would begin. Instead, Laureano arrived.

When Nedra drowned so mysteriously, and with a new child at home, the people of the village agreed that it was the most startling tragedy anyone could remember. The only facts known were that the baby had been sleeping at home while Lenny worked on the roof and Nedra went for a walk that she never returned from. Her body was found nearly a day later where the Rio Tortuga empties into the warm sea. A noisy gathering of birds helped searchers find her. Since the river was swollen from seasonal rain, it was first assumed that Nedra slipped on the bank and washed away. She was known to gather wild flowers near the water. But a dark rumor soon surfaced that Nedra had been depressed and might have jumped.

Lenny gave no credence to such a notion from the outset. Publicly he hadn't wavered. Privately, however, he remembered Nedra's odd behavior at times after the baby came. Her distant expression, her inability to sleep, her mutterings at night. He was not the sort to believe in dreams, but he couldn't deny the persistence of his darkest: as he surprises his wife at the river she looks at him without recognition and steps into the rolling water. Still, he didn't believe her capable of suicide and never would.

Nedra's mother was a humorless widow named Jacinta. For the first months after the drowning she lived in Lenny's house and provided childcare. Lenny was shattered, and the arrangement with Jacinta was necessary. Slowly, he was able to resume his work as a fisherman of spiny lobster, queen conch, and sea bass. When Jacinta went home she took the baby along, with Lenny's reluctant approval. But he soon discovered the arrangement was adding to his misery instead of helping his broken heart mend. He made plans to bring Laureano back. He wanted her there when he awoke each morning.

The hired girl, Remedios, came from one of the poorest families in the village. At seventeen she was dark-eyed and youthfully attractive. Her father was glad to accept a small payment from Lenny to permit her to live with him and care for the baby. The village gossip was immediate and predictable. Lenny chose to ignore it. But the sting of gossip so soon after losing her daughter was more than Jacinta could ignore. She asked that Remedios be sent home even though she didn't believe Lenny and the girl were intimate. No agreement could be bargained.

"I will not see my granddaughter again until that girl is gone," Jacinta said.

"I need my daughter with me where she belongs," Lenny told her. "I cannot get up in the morning otherwise. And I cannot care for her alone."

The family rift made the village gossip bolder.

* * *

Lenny was finishing the biscuit and watching the butterflies drift by the window when he heard another squeal from Laureano. He closed his eyes and saw Nedra's lovely face. His memory was clear and calm, although his eyelids twitched. Nedra had spoken frequently about the "baby blues" with her mother after Laureano was born, and her mother had talked about Nedra's moods. Lenny had heard the term *postpartum depression* but he didn't understand how a woman could feel sadness after undergoing childbirth and giving a new person life. He also remembered how she told him the pregnancy had fooled her.

"I thought my body felt the change coming," she said, "but instead of a grandmother I am becoming a mother again. It makes me feel strange, trapped in a way."

Lenny considered this statement as he tried to hold Nedra's face in his daydream. He asked her out loud: "Did you walk into the water or fall?" She didn't answer. A commotion outside brought him back to the moment. He stood up slowly and rubbed his eyes.

He washed out his cup and spoke briefly to Remedios, then walked past the simple block and stucco structures that were the homes of his neighbors. The buildings were painted a rainbow of pastels and exhibited varying stages of salty-air decomposition. He strolled the short distance to the village center, where a dozen children were excitedly proclaiming, like town criers, the day of the butterflies.

Within minutes the village square had taken on the atmosphere of a carnival. Only the men already out fishing were missing from the crowd that gathered. Four men set up a domino table beside the road, close to the butterfly swarm moving past, and spoke quietly to each other about the invasion. Women gestured dramatically to each other, as if they were performing a Greek tragedy, and watched the children chase butterflies. Several of them were sewing as they spoke. The men and women formed separate groups. Nedra's mother, Jacinta, arrived. She crossed her arms over her chest and said little. Gatekeeper strolled slowly toward the men, smiling behind a blizzard of silvery wings. Lenny issued blanket greetings, first to the women and then to the men.

A man who formed bricks by hand and dried them in the sun spoke to the village mayor: "What do you make of this, Don Roberto?" The light-skinned, pockmarked Don Roberto was quick to flash an irresistible grin. His Spaniard-in-the-woodpile bloodline and good humor kept him popular as mayor. His friends called him *paloma blanca*—white dove—in the teasing way islanders joke about their own color consciousness. "César," Don Roberto would tease back, comparing the agitator to a popular singer who was very dark and of pure African ancestry.

"*Qué maravilla!* Is it not wonderful?" Don Roberto replied. "I proclaim today a holiday. No school and no siesta. We will watch the children and the butterflies and enjoy life. I myself will provide a bottle of rum."

The brickmaker chuckled. "Ah, that is why we love our mayor," he said. "He never misses a chance to taste rum or avoid working. Reelect him right now." The other men signaled their approval with laughter.

Don Roberto laughed hardest of all; he took a deep breath and his expression became serious. He turned to the oldest man in the village, a man who was educated and wise. "What do you make of these butterflies, Great-grandfather?" The habit—becoming a custom—in the village was to seek an elder's opinion on matters of importance. Sometimes a small fee was collected.

"I have ideas about the meaning of it all," the old man said. "Would this qualify for payment?"

"It cries out for compensation," Lenny said without a hint of sarcasm. "Ideas have more value if they are paid for. Few people know the meaning of something like this."

A hat was passed. A few *centavos* dropped in. The gratuity was poured into the ancient, spotted hand. As his earnest interpretation began, all eyes were on Great-grandfather's weathered face.

"We are not so far removed from these butterflies as we think," he began. He spoke in a frail voice that required effort to hear. "God works in ways we are not equipped to decipher. The butterflies are real. They are also not real. They may at once be simple insects while also being symbols. Someone who studies bugs would tell us they are moving in such a swarm to survive, because their numbers have exceeded the food supply. But there is much more if you care to see it.

"Each butterfly contains the spirit of someone who has traveled through life before us. Some are ancestor spirits of long ago, Carib Indians who walked the islands before the Spanish or the pirate Drake sailed here. That was a simpler time. Perhaps a better time. Before the huge banyan trees in our square had even sprouted, before anyone had thought of growing cows and eating them, back when time itself was slower.

"Other butterflies are our deceased relatives and loved ones of more recent times. They mingle with the souls of Columbus himself, the captains of slave ships, the dictator Trujillo, and all who have gone before us."

Great-grandfather paused. He bit his lower lip. The others didn't speak for fear he wasn't finished. After a silence that was beginning to seem awkward, he nodded his head, blinked his tired eyes, and said to no one in particular, "*Cuál es tu opinión?*"

Everyone spoke at once. Favorable opinions of the old man's interpretations were universal. Lenny found it comforting to imagine Nedra's soul as a butterfly. She was gentle, fragile, and beautiful. He looked at the insects continuing to stream unabated and selected a single butterfly to follow as far as he could, until he lost her. The mayor went into his home nearby. The pale blue-and-yellow house embodied the appealing decrepitude that pervades Caribbean villages. He returned to the men's group displaying a mischievous smile and a large bottle of dark rum.

* * *

The moist morning evaporated as the sun climbed higher and demanded to be noticed. A comfortable lassitude settled over the village square. Women sat in the shade and worked on a cooperative sewing project that had gained importance. They gossiped in rapid and colloquial speech, glancing up now and then to confirm that the vast queue of butterflies continued coming.

Two children managed to each capture a butterfly and hold it up by the wings for the others to examine. This display, plus the gathering heat, combined to suppress the children's activity level. Two groups of olive faces pressed forward to see the specimens and nod approval. An older boy with glasses spoke in a professorial tone about aspects of butterfly anatomy. He cleared his throat and pointed his finger like a young lepidopterist leading a field trip as he described the insect's life cycle of egg, larva, pupa, and adult. He knew his subject well. "See the antennae," he said. "They are connected to the head, which connects to the thorax, which connects to the abdomen. And like all insects, they have six legs." The other children looked and listened with admiration.

Across the square two men raised their voices, bickering lightheartedly over who played the worst game of dominoes. The needling interrupted Lenny's reverie. He sat in a pensive mood in the shade of a kiosk with flaking green paint. The tiny business sold Coca-Cola, peeled oranges, and bottles of Presidente beer. Lenny looked across the road and raised his chin at his mother-in-law, Jacinta. She looked back steadily at him but gave no sign of reconciliation. He sucked the juice from a sweet orange while waiting his turn on the circumnavigating rum bottle. When the domino debate quieted he closed his eyes and let thoughts of Nedra wash over him again.

He saw her hand. It was small but not frail, curving around a glass of banana colada. He saw her face and for a moment did not breathe. His cheeks felt hot. He thought about death. Though he knew it was not to be completely understood, he decided it had to be that the dead simply pass through a wall that divides them forever from the living. He heard Nedra whistling a random charm of notes, then humming an unwritten song as she made coffee. He felt his center was gone, that if he looked down at his stomach there would be an open hole.

Lenny's mouth tightened as he continued to revisit pleasant scenes he could summon, scenes with Nedra that contrasted sharply to the monotony of his present life. Every day since her death seemed the same, each hour imbedded with the cancer of grief that stuck in his throat as if he'd swallowed spines from his lobsters. Nights were worse. He could only observe life. Participation was impossible except to put forth a good front for other people. He moved about randomly and did what needed to be done, but no more. He thought every day about the dream where she didn't know him and stepped into the water. He pictured Nedra after the baby came and was forced to again acknowledge sleepless nights, sudden melancholy, troubled expressions that might have masked dark thoughts.

Lenny rose, stretched, and walked to the edge of the road to stand close to the stream of butterflies. His somber mood lifted as three children joined him, crossing their wrists and mimicking wings with their hands.

"I will no longer choke my mind with unhappy things, Nedra," he said aloud but to himself. "I will be forty-six years old, and it is time to embrace life and be a good father. I will not dwell on how I cursed God and prayed to him at the same time. I will allow this day and these lovely creatures flying past and these children to mark a new beginning. I will remember the strength in your arms when you made bread. I will remember your face when we made love. I will remember how you could read my mind and how your neck curved where it met your shoulder. Not every day is the same."

* * *

The bright sun had crossed its zenith and shadows were growing longer when the butterfly stream began to separate. A woman with thinning white hair and parchment skin pointed to the sky. The villagers and jabbering children began to inventory the growing number of birds in the sky.

A dozen or more frigate birds glided in lazy circles. Their black wings contrasted sharply with the pure-white cattle egrets perched in trees. Herons, kites, and cormorants perched randomly in the limbs and on rooftops. All the birds seemed to watch, with interest, the swirling string of buffet items passing along the road.

Dogs barked. Cats hissed. Geckos and chameleons normally paralytically sluggish in early afternoon sat alert on fences and rocks.

The men observed the excitements and were more talkative than usual. A man wearing a red baseball cap waved the rum bottle and declared it a dead soldier. A shy young farmer who spoke so seldom his voice was eggshell brittle, uncharacteristically said with force: "*Dios*. Look. What have they made?" The men looked where he pointed, toward the sewing klatch.

"*Madre Santa*, it is huge," Lenny said.

"Why do we need a tent?" said the mayor.

"No, no," the shy farmer corrected. "It is a butterfly trap. They have made a snare."

The women were hoisting and unfolding a breadth of makeshift material. Gauze, cheesecloth, rags, and swatches of muslin and cotton were sewn together to form a rough rectangle of twenty-five-by-fifteen feet. They smiled and gave directions to one another as they spread their creation. All gathered to see the handiwork on the ground. Lenny intentionally stood next to Nedra's mother Jacinta. She did not look up or move away.

"What is it for?" the brickmaker asked his wife. "Our windows are not big enough for this curtain." Several of the men laughed because the rum made everything funny.

"Do not be ridiculous," said Matilda, a woman whose lush body formed no sharp angles and whose caramel face was round and pretty. She smiled. "As anyone can see, this is a fine butterfly trap."

"I have a grand idea," proclaimed Mayor Don Roberto. "We will catch many of these butterflies and arrange them on the cloth to make a picture of our great politician, El Presidente. We will use other colorful bugs for his eyes and hair and dark ones for his mustache. It will be a bug portrait of a bug!"

"*Basta*. Stop it," Matilda said, adjusting her flowered dress of an undetermined size. "I started this project, and it is going to work." She motioned to her two sons. "Let us get it up."

The twin banyan trees that marked the center of the village sat on either side of the road and had been in place for nearly four hundred years. They were impressively tall but shocking in girth. In a custom that was older than anyone could remember, young people assessed their own growth by locking hands and trying to reach around one of the tree trunks. They were in their midteens or older before six of them could accommodate the circumference.

The trees were easy to climb; the trunks were fitted with knots and knobs and wrinkles that made perfect handholds and footholds. Matilda's sons were twenty feet high in seconds and a cord was tossed up to one of them. He tied off his end and threw the cord to his brother in the other tree, who completed the line and called for the sheet of mismatched material. The trap was tied to the anchor cord, then secured to the ground with flat stones. After adjustments from Matilda plus the soft wind billowing the cloth, the banyan trees sported a delicate sail. Everyone backed away to see what would happen.

Lenny had left the gathering for a few minutes but now returned with Laureano in his arms and Remedios close behind. The butterfly stream had thinned but hundreds still drifted through the square. When the people backed away and stood quietly, the nearly transparent material didn't alarm the migrating insects. With people, birds, dogs, cats, and lizards watching, first one, then two, then a dozen butterflies flew into the snare, became gently entangled, and fell to the ground.

"It works," Matilda shouted with pride. "Look at that. We are butterfly collectors. Children, put them in boxes before they fly away."

"What on earth will they do with them, Matilda?" the brickmaker asked, as surprised as the other adults that the trap worked at all.

"What does it matter. Look at the fun they are having."

Matilda was correct. The village children of all ages, from those barely walking to the teenagers who normally scorned activities not of their own invention, were pitching in to collect bugs. Once, an entire squadron floated into the net and the laughing children plucked them like flowers and put them into a box that had materialized.

After several minutes nearly all the butterflies avoided the makeshift material. No one would offer an explanation for how they did this. The boys shimmied back up the banyans and dropped the snare to the ground.

Grandmother Esteban, whose mind had acquired a noticeable drift, spoke up to the assembly: "*Escúchame.* This has happened before. I remember when I was a young girl how the butterflies came through by the tens of thousands."

The adults exchanged skeptical glances, believing Señora Esteban to be cloudy on the subject but wanting to hear more. "What happened?" someone asked. "Did you catch them?"

"Yes, we did. We could catch them with our hands in those days. We were faster and more determined than children today. When you are young, everything is possible. It's only when we get older that pessimism comes. I remember putting them in a potato sack."

"What did you do with them, Grandmother?" The questioner was Matilda again.

The old woman paused, looked at her shoes, then closed her eyes and said in a small voice: "I believe we made an excellent soup. Very milky and sweet."

Lenny saw an opportunity and took it. He raised his arms over his head and displayed his palms. "My neighbors," he said with volume. "I am no speechmaker, but let me say something to you. The butterflies have brought us together, so this is the time." He took three steps to stand beside Remedios, who held his daughter on her shoulder. "I know there has been gossip because I brought this young woman into my house to care for Laureano. I blame only myself for such talk. But I wish to make clear the truth, which is that she is only there for the baby. Let me say it again. Remedios is only there to care for the baby. There is nothing else. I ask for your tolerance and understanding because suspicion has caused a problem in my family." Lenny took his daughter from Remedios and put her around his neck. "Thank you for listening to me."

A murmur of approval spread quickly. Lenny was receiving unanimous praise for his declaration when Gatekeeper shouted, "Look! They're going between the trees again."

The boys had rehung the snare and a new phalanx of butterflies was drifting lazily into the net. Reenergized children resumed their collecting duties. Small hands were dropping creatures into the box again when, alarmingly, an urgent shriek rang out, heard by all.

"That was little Pablo," the mayor said. "*Dios,* it sounds like something scared him." But it was worse. Six-year-old Pablo's feelings had been hurt.

"They will not fly!" he wailed between sobs. "They cannot fly anymore."

Pablo's twin sister was the first to grasp the problem and her lamentations soon matched her brother's. "Turn them loose!" she cried. "*No pueden volar!* They cannot fly!"

An investigation determined that little Pablo had attempted to set the collected butterflies free, but when he turned the box over and dropped the creatures to the ground they toppled from side to side or laid unmoving where they fell. The children's handling had done its damage. Only two flew away. The collecting stopped at once. The children were quiet, even the older ones.

At that moment, and as if on cue, the afternoon rain began. One of only two clouds passing over the sky managed to weep a fine mist. When some of the youngest children continued sobbing a man produced the machete he used in the sugarcane fields and held it aloft. "Cut it down!" he shouted.

Pablo and his sister were given the first cuts at the gauzy material with an adult steering the machete. The children took turns slicing. The teenagers were last, cutting higher and higher until the trap was in shreds and falling down.

The two clouds became one. The rain was still gentle but had to be noticed. The villagers divided into families and left the square, looking back to see two women gathering the snare material. With the raindrops, the butterfly stream thinned and then disappeared. Within minutes the only butterflies to be seen were the dead and the dying under the banyan trees. Those, and the ones Grandmother Esteban took home in her apron.

Jacinta didn't leave right away. She looked directly at Lenny. He held Laureano out to her. She took her granddaughter and kissed her on the cheek. Remedios stood quietly nearby.

"You were strong to say those things to everyone," Jacinta said to her son-in-law. She was nervous, and one hand comforted the other as she held Laureano in the crook of her arm.

"I meant every word. This day was changed by the butterflies. Now we need to change. We both know Nedra would not abide tension between us."

"Then let us go cook some fish."

"Remedios goes too."

Jacinta paused, but only for a moment. "I know. I know. *Vamonos.*"

As the villagers retreated into their warren of modest homes, the day of the butterflies morphed into routine activities and the smell of coffee, garlic, and chickpeas.

Grandmother Esteban decocted a pot of butterfly soup from her imagined memory of the dish. The effort was cloudy and smelled bitter. She looked at it closely and sniffed, then dipped her finger and licked it. Her face strongly disapproved. She threw the liquid out and never spoke of it again. As the soup went out the back window, several ordinary scenes played out around the village.

Matilda and her sons talked and laughed as she cooked. The younger son shaped a makeshift baseball by wadding a pair of holey socks and covering the round wad with white tape. When her sons sat down to eat, Matilda stood behind them and recited a short prayer.

Gatekeeper lifted his barrier across the lane and sat it down. He knew no one was coming through at dusk. For a moment, he wished for more butterflies the next day but quickly knew better and went inside.

Mayor Don Roberto opened a third beer and spoke with affection to his wife. "A fine day. Yes, indeed, a fine day. Would you like some of this before we eat, my dear?"

Great-grandfather sat in a splintery chair and smoked a short pipe. He thought about his interpretation of the day's events and how he had spoken. He said out loud: "I should have said the soul of Christopher Columbus himself was leading the butterflies; I will make sure they know tomorrow."

The young farmer with an eggshell voice, who lived alone after his parents died four months apart, cut a sweet potato and thought about one of the village girls he had watched. She was fifteen, going on thirty.

Jacinta cuddled Laureano as she walked to Lenny's home beside him. Remedios followed the unhurried procession. Lenny thought about the day's work left undone and was at ease that he didn't care. He put his arm around his mother-in-law's shoulders and said: "Sometimes I dream that she is jumping into the water. Do you think it is even possible?"

"Anything is possible," Jacinta replied in a sorrowful tone. "But I really do not think so."

Lenny looked her in the eyes: "I have vowed to think only the best of her. If we both do that maybe she will be at peace."

Inside the house, Nedra's resourceful decorations were in evidence. The patterned rug beneath the table had given her joy, as had the yellow curtains she made. Her clothes were still in a black trunk in the corner. On a wall hung Lenny's homemade clock with its hands of recycled fan blades. The house was clean and presented an air of simple dignity.

They ate especially well that evening. Black bean soup, rice, and pan-seared sea bass with a sauce based on toasted coconut. Laureano got tiny pieces of the fish with rice and milk. Lenny took down the picture of Nedra from the shelf to give his guests a closer look. He showed pictures of their two grown children. When Jacinta excused herself to walk home and Remedios prepared the child for bed, Lenny thought about what would need to be done the next morning. Quite early, he would check his lobster pots and fish for more sea bass.

He cleared the table and stacked the dishes beside a small sink. He took a handful of fish bones and walked outside to deposit them in the compost near his garden.

The dying wind made a sighing sound as it passed invisibly over the grass. Despite his effort to keep such thoughts at bay, he wondered if Nedra had felt like the snared butterflies—trapped and unable to fly. If so, should he have seen it?

He looked out through the moonless night across the dark water of the sea.

He heard a snap and looked down at his hand as if it belonged to someone else. He watched it close tighter and tighter against the sharp fish bones until he saw blood trickling in his palm. Fidel Lenin Medina felt nothing. He looked again at the ocean water, breaking in white waves against the island shore. Slowly, he threw the bones into the heap.

FAKE-NEWS CHRISTMAS LETTER #2

Dear Friends,

It was the best of times. It was the best of times. Yet again we've had a wonderful year and feel the need to reach out, to share.

You may recall from the previous Christmas letter that we had eliminated stress from our daily activities and fat from our diets, but there was still the guilt from allowing ourselves the occasional piece of broiled fish. So we reached into that vast reservoir of willpower we all possess to simplify even further. We now eat only root vegetables and organic raw fruit washed in rainwater. Once a month we have dessert—a quarter cup of brown rice sweetened with maple sap we collect ourselves and reduce to a light syrup.

On the beverage front, all studies show the correlation between modest wine consumption and vigorous health so we judiciously consume two glasses of 1927 Hungarian Tokaji Aszú daily—unfiltered, of course. To augment our dietary discipline we take a wide range of vitamins and supplements to boost our intake of beta-carotene, selenium, zinc, coenzyme Q10, and melatonin.

We also stepped up our exercise regimen this year. Jeff is in full preparation for the next Heart of America marathon with an ambition toward Boston by running about one hundred miles each week. Rebekah has become a certified step-aerobics instructor. She's in negotiations with E.S.P.N. to star in an exercise-based drama series to be called **Flatbelly and Rockbuns.**

Savannah is now three years old and becoming ever more fluent in Spanish, French, and Japanese. She started gymnastics, of course, with an eye toward gold in the Olympics a decade or so from now. We hired a brace of unemployed Russian coaches for her private training. The progress is remarkable. We've been contacted by a nationally known sports agent who has produced a seven-figure advance for an endorsement contract with Nike, but so far we've turned it down. It just doesn't feel in keeping with the true spirit of amateurism.

Cooper Charles has arrived. Can you believe it? He's already nearly a year old! His pediatrician said he'd not seen nor heard of a baby who slept from 8 p.m. to 8 a.m. the first night home and every night since. But what surprised us even more are the dry diapers. The little guy mumbles "ca-ca" and we hold him over the potty and he voids by himself. Also, we credit strong genetics for the fact that after his initial exam the doctor said he wouldn't need the usual inoculations. No doubt he won't miss the needles.

Son Gabriel completed his tour of duty with the Peace Corps digging wells in Rwanda and was elected a Rhodes scholar for a year of study at Oxford. His callings are the translation of ancient Sumerian texts and the composition of New Age music.

Jeff continues to paint and sculpt. His next showing in London is scheduled for the spring. Rebekah's volunteer work advising the local road and bridge department to ensure structural integrity fills her spare time.

At this time of joy and celebration we wish you the best of everything.

A VERY MERRY CHRISTMAS!

WHEN FATHER HIT MOTHER

When father hit mother I was big-boy eight.
Ike was in.
Sissy and Bud, diapery and wee,
                    dreamt and sweated upstairs.

Something gurgled inside me as I charged him.
An ursine growl? A curse from a child? Rage?
I tackled a knee, hard for eight, but his hot anger was deep
                    and midwifed in the Great Depression.

He threw me back, hard for thirty-eight, silent and dangerous.
The coffee table skidded. My shin skin was skinned—violated.
                    A ceramic ballerina landed broken nearby.

Mother stayed, as Mamie did with Ike. We grew up,
                    as children do, though sometimes
                    caught in the
                    awkward limbo of her silence.
                    The effluvium of martyrdom.

Now he is gone, leaving much. She too is gone,
whinnying no more.

> Revenge was forsworn in favor of decades
> dripping with holidays and determined
> reunions.

A glued dancer cannot speak.

We pretend not to remember.

Presidents have come and gone, and I am big-boy senior.

Still, I think of it and my shin throbs.

BIRD AND WINDOW
(MATING SEASON)

Flutter, flutter, thump.
You've done it this time, little bluebird, tiny hero.
Your kamikaze dive into my window may be fatal, but
not divine wind.

I'd come outside if I could, where you lie supine
Breathing shallowly.
I'd massage your tiny chest,
De-concuss your tiny head
And give you mouth-to-beak
If I could.

But there's West Nile virus
And survival of the fittest
To consider.

In the instant before your calamity could you see
It was you,

Not some overdressed, disingenuous rival displaying
To your mate?
Too late to swerve or brake.

Attention, you who have glanced into a glass,
Come face to face with a copy of yourself,
Twisted your head for a better angle
And contemplated your inadequacies.
Forgive yourself and go with grace.

Sleep on, tough guy, winged hero.
Dream of her, of soaring in the clouds,
Of ripe berries, fat grasshoppers.
Then, we hope, awaken,
Totter a moment,
Chirrup
And fly away.

GETTING EVEN

The first thing Dilly sees when he squints through the door of Wayne's double-wide is little Trina crawling on the floor and playing with what looks like a Sig Sauer 9mm pistol. "Perfect," he mutters as he leans through the door. "Wonder if it's loaded." He sees his brother's wife asleep on a tired yellow couch. In her limp hand is an empty Smirnoff bottle.

"Jesus, Mary, and Joseph," Dilly whispers as he steps inside. "This place smells like cigarettes and puke." He grabs the pistol from the two-year-old and lays it on the TV. A silencer lies on a shelf nearby. Trina immediately cries to get it back. Jolene opens one eye and groans as she raises up from the couch. Her roundish face is red on one side where it was buried. She sits up and little pains flash through her eyes so she squints them closed and opened a few times. She manages a deep breath and says: "What the hell are you doing here, Dilly?" She crumples into the back of the couch. "Haven't seen you in a year."

"Hey there, Jolene. Wayne called me from jail." Dilly opens a window and turns off *Oprah*. "He's got big problems and needs help." Dilly moves to the trailer's kitchen sink and looks unsuccessfully for a clean water glass. "He says some guy set him up. Some pony-tailed, Chardonnay-drinking movie guy." Dilly picks up Trina. "Hey, you, little creamy. You've really grown." Trina lobster-claws his nose and tries to dive for the gun. "You're quick, little pepper pot," Dilly growls into her neck. "Gimme a kiss right here."

"I know all about it," Jolene says, trying to light a butt from the ashtray. "This guy is some kind of producer. He's a B-lister but he has all the A-listers in his phone. He's not Mister Big, but he probably knows him. Wayne should've left you out of it."

"Why's that?"

"Because you went the hell off to Arizona and used your good looks to get a straight life. You still working on that golf course or country club or whatever? You still got that beautiful girlfriend? You got out of old Shakeytown in one piece and your brother ought not drag you back. L.A. still sucks."

"Jolene, you sound worse off than Wayne."

"Better believe it. I get chest pains in the night. My dog barks and the neighbors yell. Look how this little girl is into everything. And I drink too much. If you cut my toe, vodka runs out." Jolene sticks a smudgy juice bottle into Trina's mouth.

"He said he's in jail for drugs again but not just for possession," Dilly says. "They cut his phone call off before he could tell me everything."

"Yep. What else? This time he got caught selling to a narc. He's still on probation for possession, so I guess they'll send him to prison."

"He was able to tell me this movie dude nailed him to the cross to save his own hide."

"Worse than that. The guy begged him to get a bag of coke within an hour. Wayne wasn't really selling, just using. The Hollywood guy claimed his girlfriend was going to blow the whistle to his wife and ruin his life unless he got her some coke right now. Wayne hadn't seen this guy for months and barely knew him through some real coke dealer. Mr. B-List was shielding his own dealer and setting Wayne up. Offered him three times the going price, then brought the lady narc into it and had Wayne sell to her and claimed everything was fine, that the lady was taking it to his girlfriend. We needed the money. He was toast."

"What do you think Wayne wants me to do?"

"I'd tell you if I knew. He knows he can always count on you. Says you've never turned him down when he needed help."

"I guess that's about right. He's still my big brother."

"Yeah, I know. I still think he ought to leave you be. And you ought to climb back in that big Silverado and head east back to Phoenix."

"Why do you say that, Jolene?"

"'Cause even though he claimed he was trying to do better he was screwing up again. First it was just a couple beers. He promised to stop. Then two or three of them that work together for the landscaper got to drinking Jim

Beam. I could smell it on him when he got home. He'd lie about it, but I could tell. He gets quiet, but there's mean in his eyes when he drinks whiskey. I gave up myself about then and got back on vodka. Then he was snorting. Not that much, but it was enough. I wasn't surprised when the cops came knocking."

"And you really don't know what he wants me to do? Maybe bail him out?"

"Got no idea. Maybe that's it. But then you ought to shake his hand and drive away. It's OK to keep your distance. Maybe if he did go to prison he'd come out better."

"You may be right, Jolene. But I drove all this way, so the least I can do is go see him and find out what's on his mind."

* * *

The Los Angeles County Jail is clean, modern, efficient, and crowded. When Dilly arrives to visit Wayne the receptionist smiles through thick lipstick and pecks her computer keys before sending him onward.

"I knew you'd come, Dilly," Wayne says through the hole in the plexiglass window. "When you were born I said you were a dilly, and you still are. I'm glad nobody calls you William Lee." Wayne is wearing an orange jumpsuit and flip-flops.

"Hey there, Wayne Cooper." Dilly looks down the row of windows where two guys are trying to kiss each other through the talk hole. "You OK?"

"I've been better." Wayne settles his slender frame into a cheap plastic chair and combs his hair with his fingers.

"I hear that. This sounds like a genuine screw job. Jolene told me a little."

"Mister Movie Big Shot put me in a box. He not only lied through his teeth, he sawed me in half and watched my guts run out. You got to help me get even, Dilly. I'm going down but this scum needs to pay."

Dilly scoots his chair closer to the window. He glances in the direction of the disinterested guard, a Clydesdale in a cop suit with eyes that meant to be shut but hadn't gotten around to it. Wayne begins to explain what he's thinking. A tingling in Dilly's foot like there's a beetle trapped in his shoe begins, along with a sense of stopped time as his own big brother asks him to take a gun and shoot some dork in the knee. Dilly's face looks like the King of Hearts in a card deck, expressionless and therefore profound, all-knowing, judgmental.

"I'm not saying kill him," Wayne says. "I just can't think of anything else. Art Spiegel thinks only of Art Spiegel. He's a con man with a snow cone for a heart. He needs to pay up for what he's done to me. I've got this pistol at home with a silencer."

"Yeah, bro. I've seen it. Your daughter thinks it's a toy. I took it away from her and put it in my truck."

"Sounds like Jolene's drinking again instead of paying attention. She's a good mom when she's sober. But with me gone and in a jam she'll drink like a carp all day. She quit for a while, then started again because I messed up."

"Wayne, I've got my life squared away. My job's not bad, and my girlfriend loves me. I love her back. I'm not much of a candidate to go commit a felony, even for you."

"The last thing I want to do is lean on my little brother. I just don't know what else there is. This guy has ripped me a new one. Ruined my life. Since the day I tackled you and kept that trash truck from turning you into a grease spot, you've said you'll never turn me down."

Dilly tilts his chair onto its back legs and locks his hands behind his neck. "I'm not saying I'm turning you down, but just think what you're asking. Do you want my life ruined too? I'm supposed to go up to some guy and shoot him in the leg? If I'm caught, they'll put me in with that guy down there trying to kiss his boyfriend."

Wayne rolls his eyes. "That's James. He gets out today. His buddy got him arrested for assault, but now he won't press charges or testify. They've made up, as you can see. James had him handcuffed while they were doing whatever they do, but got too rough and sent him to the walk-in clinic to get patched up. Said he got carried away."

"Lovely story," Dilly says. "Right up there with *Snow White*."

Wayne lowers his voice and quietly speaks through the talk hole. "There's no way you'll get caught. You have no connection with Mister B-List and you're in Arizona. You follow him to somewhere quiet, maybe a parking lot or to his gated entry. Then you shoot Arthur in the knee or the leg, point-blank, and drop him like a bad transmission. Tell him if he calls the police, he and his girlfriend are front-page in the *L.A. Times*, especially how he keeps her in coke. If that happens, he's done. Tell him to get his leg fixed and come visit me in jail. I'll tell him you were a mob guy from San Diego, and I'm connected so he better get me the best lawyer who can get me probation. That's the end of it. You're back in Arizona."

"Anything that sounds so simple won't be," Dilly says, looking Wayne in the eye. "Cops aren't stupid. Hospitals have to report gunshot wounds. I understand you'd like to stay out of prison by getting probation, but a lot of things would have to go just right for that to happen."

"Dilly, I'm damned if I can come up with anything else. I been thinking about it ever since he hustled me. I know Arthur's a little coward. Some serious muscle could turn this around. He's got more money than brains. I was there and got sucked in. Sure, that's my fault. But if I could stay out of prison, I could tell him his other leg will get shot unless he hands over some dough to get me and Jolene and Trina set up to move to Seattle. Jolene's got some family there, and I'd sure like to start over.

"The Academy Awards are tomorrow night, my brother. Arthur will be there. Here, look at his picture from this magazine clipping of some big party. All you'd have to do is follow him when he leaves and stick the gun in his face and then his leg when he gets to his home gate. I can even tell you where he lives in case you lose him."

* * *

Which is why Dilly finds himself driving slowly through a middle-class neighborhood not far from downtown Los Angeles, California, in the middle of a warm, end-of-February day with his head full of bumblebees. He's not lost, but he's certainly taking the long way back to Wayne's trailer park. He is thinking about the times his big brother bailed him out of trouble of one kind or another as they were growing up poor in Arkansas. *Sure,* he's thinking, *he saved my life outright when I didn't see that truck coming. And there were many other times not so dramatic when I needed help and he was there. No one ever messed with me because they knew if they did, Wayne would be coming around. The most important thing he did was protect me from Dad the best he could. He actually tried to fight the old man, the drunken abuser who couldn't keep a job. Several times he got his ass kicked defending me. Now he wants me to shoot someone. Christ.*

* * *

Now Dilly is walking aimlessly through the trailer park, lost in the folds of his own cerebral cortex, when he finds himself talking to a man who says he is Jahmer Cedar from South Dakota.

"How do, Mister Cedar," Dilly says. "No, I don't live here. I'm just visiting."

"Well, shoot. But that's plenty lucky for you. A handsome boy with a full head of hair and straight teeth shouldn't live in a clumpy dumpy like this. Houses don't supposed to have wheels." Dilly realizes the man is one sandwich short of a picnic and remembers why he escaped L.A. The place will drive you nuts.

Dilly looks at Mr. Cedar and the tight-haired little dog alongside him with an expressionless but pleasant stare, like he might look at a dragonfly on a lily pad, waiting to see what happens next. Before Dilly can break away and resume his stroll he learns several things about his new friend: why he always wears a red flannel shirt, why he stopped clipping his ear hair, how the bad weather takes half your crop when you farm in South Dakota, and the names, ages, and locations of his immediate family members. The dog gives Dilly his escape moment. It crouches and trembles, straining to make a doggy pile. Mr. Cedar baby-talks the dog and pulls a putty knife and baggy from his pocket, using the putty knife as a meticulous butt wiper and the baggy to hold the mess. Dilly waves good-bye and flees to Jolene and Trina.

The TV screen is filled with angry audience members berating a panel of teenagers dressed in grunge. The teens are defending self-mutilation as they display their nose rings, tongue studs, and eyelid and lip piercings. Tattoos are everywhere. Trina is lying on the floor watching. Jolene is unwrapping frozen lasagna.

"Hey, Jolene," Dilly asks, "should she be watching this?"

"It makes her sleepy for a nap. She won't watch *Sesame Street*. I know she don't understand, but they sure got some odd ones on TV nowadays."

* * *

Late afternoon the next day Dilly is driving again. The loaded pistol is in his belt, underneath his loose camp shirt. It's not heavy because instead of a Sig Sauer, it turns out it's a cheap knockoff of a Russian Makarov 9mm, readily available for a hundred bucks. He is smiling at the Silverado's thrum because he remembers his girlfriend's taunt about the old pickup he had when they first met. She said the old truck was so underpowered that it slowed down when you turned the radio on. Dilly has no idea what he is going to do, if anything. He is driving toward the Dolby Theatre, where the Oscars are to be held later that evening. Traffic is light, considering he's in L.A., because it's Sunday.

A quarter mile from the theater traffic thickens and stops because of an accident scene. Red and yellow lights twirl. A traffic cop has his motorcycle parked sideways to block the street and waves Dilly and other cars to a side street. Dilly finds a spot to park and walks back to get a closer look and kill time. An ambulance is being loaded with two injured men, both of them dressed in white. Next to Dilly stands an agitated man in a white chef's jacket and slicked-back hair, who says, to no one in particular: "This is it. I'm ruined. There's no way. This is it." The man is close to tears.

"Hey there, buddy, take it easy." Dilly feels sorry for the guy. "Were you in this wreck?"

"I wish I had been." His voice trembles. "I wish they were hauling me away. That's two of my best waiters, gone for the night. I'm in charge of the catering for the Oscars, and now I'm dead in the water. They called me when they got hit by the truck."

"Just try to calm down. Your guys don't seem to be hurt bad."

"No, but they're bruised and skinned up and can't work tonight. I've got no time to find help." The guy gives Dilly an appraising look. "Hey, you're a nice-looking young guy. You ever been a waiter? All you'd have to do is walk around with a tray. Generous pay, in cash, and you'll see a herd of famous people. No application or ID needed. Could you work a few hours, starting right now?"

* * *

Which is why Dilly finds himself in a bathroom putting on a waiter's outfit twenty-five minutes later. Gray silk slacks and a pearl-white jacket with an Oscar statuette embroidered on the front. The pistol is now tucked in the belt of his new pants because the head caterer pulled Dilly right past the back entrance security guard. "No sweat, Bob," the chef said to the guard. "We're in a rush, and he's with me."

Dilly shuddered as they swept past. He realized what might have happened had he been searched or forced through a metal detector. The catering chef has departed. Dilly is to dress and get a crash course from a headwaiter. His job will be easy. He's simply to follow an assigned route through the early guests, who bunch up like cattle in the reception areas of the theater. He will carry lacquered trays of sushi, palm-sized plates, and napkins. He will go back to the kitchen for refills. He will smile but not grin. He will not speak to the rich and famous unless spoken to. Service will begin in about an hour and a half. Until then, he will hang with the other waiters and relax. He makes small talk, uncomfortable knowing what's stuck in his waistband and having no idea what he will or won't do. He lies and says he lives in Pasadena and sells insurance. As Dilly has heard but experiences for the first time, posing as an insurance salesman blunts curiosity. One of the waiters holds the floor on a regular basis, saying he hates his job and only does it to pay for acting classes. He still believes he'll turn out to be someone else.

The wait time passes uneventfully. Dilly thumbs a magazine in the kitchen annex and periodically escapes to the bathroom. A splash of cold water in the face and a towel from the basket keeps the nerve sweat under control. He doesn't think he's going to fire a shot in this milieu, but maybe he can spot Arthur Spiegel and follow him home. He's surprised to feel the lump in his throat and see the tears trying to form in the mirror. He's a man taking control of his life at age thirty-one after a history of beery, vomity nights; broken promises; and a love life featuring numerous women like the dance of a magnet and iron filings. Yet he finds himself packing a loaded gun at a world-famous gathering of greatly admired people. He has a sinking feeling that something is wrong, or about to go wrong. Or maybe something was always wrong. Dilly wants to be an optimist. He's adept at believing this or that will happen, and his life will be in order. Somehow, until lately, this or that has never quite happened.

"Suck it up, boy," Dilly tells the mirror while wiping his eyes and bracing himself with the time-honored, testosterone-induced protocol of suppressed male emotion. "This is for you, big brother." He adjusts the cheap 9mm and exits the bathroom with his shoulders back and his jaw set.

* * *

Harrison Ford declines the sushi. But Julia Roberts takes two chunks of ahi tuna wrapped in seaweed and rice as she tells the group hanging on her every word, "It was heaven. A four-day weekend at the tip of Baja watching the whales go by. It's a neat little hideaway with these suites hanging on a cliff above the ocean."

Sean Connery reaches toward the tray and then pulls his hand back. "What's that, sushi? No thanks. In Scotland we use that for bait."

Spielberg also declines, but standing nearby is Ryan Gosling, who takes three pieces with a modest expression and then inhales them, saying, "I'm starved." Tom Hanks is making a point to Anthony Hopkins and Liam Neeson nearby.

Dilly finishes passing out his first tray, feeling a combination of exhilaration and unease as the pistol massages his stomach. He circles through the kitchen for a second tray. As he squeezes through the double door to patrol the party he sees Arthur Spiegel. There's no mistaking him from the picture Wayne provided. He's headed for a back-of-the-house bathroom. It's not his first rodeo at the Dolby.

The episode is pure luck. Dilly knows it as he enters the bathroom a few steps behind Arthur and in a millisecond decides what to do. Mr. B-List is unzipping himself in front of a urinal. He's alone. Dilly calmly sets his sushi tray on the sink and slides out the weapon. He waves it past Arthur's face, then grabs his head by the ponytail and pulls it backward while shoving the pistol in his back. "Don't make a sound, you slimeball, if you want to walk out of here. Keep your hands on your junk." Dilly yanks the ponytail again and moves the Makarov to point at Arthur's member, which is being held tightly by trembling hands and is dribbling urine down his Armani tux and Bally shoes. "How'd you like it if I pull this trigger and blow that thing right off?" Dilly pulls the ponytail a third time and jabs the pistol.

"Oh god oh god no no no. God, Mister, what is this? What'd I do to you?"

"Shut up, you stupid ass. I told you to keep quiet. I'll do the talking. You've jacked with the wrong people. You thought you'd send Wayne to prison to save your own dealer and your own butt. You thought nothing would happen to you, that Wayne was some cokehead you could screw over. You made a big mistake." Dilly moves the pistol away from Arthur's limp shaft and jams it roughly into the back of his head. He pushes forward with the barrel.

"Wayne has friends. He's connected. His friends make your dicky-doo Hollywood pals look like dishwashers from Hooterville. I'm a professional. I'm connected. You better get that straight. If I can get to you inside the Oscars, you damn well better believe I can get to you anywhere I choose. You hear me?" Arthur shakes his head up and down. He is sobbing.

"This time you're lucky. You don't want there to be a next time. You get just one chance. I'd just as soon blow your nuts off right now, but my orders are to give you one chance to make it up to Wayne. So here's what's gonna happen. I'm gonna walk away from you. You're gonna take three minutes to clean yourself up and go back to the party. You haven't seen my face. You are not, repeat not, gonna say a word to anyone about this. We'll be watching. If you don't do exactly what I'm telling you, then you can kiss that little thing you're holding good-bye. Also, good buddy, you and the girlfriend you keep coked up will look a little rough in the *L.A. Times*.

"You're going to stay at the party for one hour. Then you'll get in your car and start making phone calls. You get the best lawyer your money can buy. Tonight, not tomorrow. You bail Wayne out of jail, and we want the charges dismissed. Whatever it takes. You get it done.

"When Wayne is out you got twenty-four hours to have an envelope delivered to him with thirty thousand dollars of your cash in it. That's the last you'll ever see of him, or me for that matter. You've still got a life. If you screw it up or get any asswipe ideas of your own, you'll see me again. And I'll be the last thing you ever see. You got it?" Dilly pushes the gun barrel harder against Arthur's neck. "Answer me. *You got it?*"

"Yes," Arthur whispers.

"Now keep your face against that wall for three minutes until I'm gone." Dilly picks up his tray and glances back to see Arthur begin to vomit a spray of expensive lunch into the urinal. Dilly is through the kitchen and out of the building carrying his civvies in less than a minute. The wiped pistol and silencer splash in a reservoir miles away as he drives exactly the speed limit out of L.A. and into a cloudless night hung with a glowing apricot moon.

* * *

Kayla is leaving for work when Dilly arrives at their tidy Phoenix apartment the next morning. "I got your note," she says. "You had to go help your brother. I missed you. I'm running a little late, but will you tell me about it tonight?"

Dilly kisses her intensely. "I missed you too. A lot. We'll talk about it later." She has left a modest table lamp turned on, and the yellow light makes the room look like an old Flemish painting. Her note is under the lamp: "I missed you, darling William." Dilly is reading when his cell phone vibrates.

"Dilly, it's me."

"Hey there, bro."

"What'd you do?"

"What do you mean?"

"I mean what did you do? I'm out of jail, and they say there won't even be charges. Some high-powered lawyer says the police entrapped me. He got me right out, and now I'm back at home. Jolene says you left in the afternoon and never came back. What'd you do?"

"Not much, Wayne. Let's just forget it. Your pistol and silencer are gone and you won't need them. I just gave Arthur a talking-to. Apparently I convinced him to do the right thing."

"Apparently you did. You must have been convincing. I got a call from a messenger service and they'll be here at two o'clock with an envelope for me. What's that all about?"

"It'll give you every chance to start over. Think about how close you came to prison and what that would have been like. You won't duck it if there's a next time. Think what's happening with Jolene and little Trina, but also what's happening with you. What do you want from life, big brother? Why don't you try clean and sober for a while? Give it a chance. Move the three of you to Seattle, where you said Jolene's got family. There are plenty of straight jobs. You might like it. Will you at least think about it?"

"Well, hell, Dilly. I been this way since we were kids. Sure, I might like to be different but I also like getting wrecked. Would I be happier? Can a guy really change or do we stay the way we are?"

"There's a price for your way, Wayne, a high price. Remember how it was with Dad? You're still fighting him, but you're mostly just like him. He told us we were bad, but we weren't. He was the bad one. Every time we try to figure out how to live he's still standing there in the way, even though he drank himself to death long ago. Would you be happier? How in hell am I supposed to know? Happiness is hard to describe, but misery can almost be touched. Can a person change? Yep. In a New York second. Ask the guy who wins the lottery or the one just diagnosed with cancer. We can change if the motivation is strong enough."

"I'm sure you're right, Dilly. Maybe the party is over. Sobriety scares me, though. A change of scenery would help. Do you think you could teach me to like it?"

"I'll try to help, bro. But to actually change your life, you'll be on your own. You'll need to be strong. Stay in touch, and good luck."

FAKE-NEWS CHRISTMAS LETTER #3

Dearest Friends,

We pause again at the holidays to be thankful for another splendid year for our family. We try to be humble, but pride in our achievements is hard to contain.

Savannah has continued her unusual intellectual development and has started first grade despite being only four years old. Her prodigal gift for languages was already clear (she's now reading Proust in French and Goethe in German), but her teacher uncovered a parallel talent in mathematics that we hadn't suspected. With only the nudge of our buying a barely used Cray supercomputer from the Department of Defense, she has developed code-breaking software that allows us, via satellite, to patch into top-secret calls in Moscow, Beijing, and Pyongyang. The DOD appreciates the help. Like most of us, though, she has trouble making a cell-phone call across the street.

Cooper is now two, and his interests have moved to snare drums and karate. Though his middle-of-the-night practicing can test one's patience and lead to groggy breakfasts, we take solace in knowing that many parents have trouble getting their children to practice their music lessons at all. And the karate seems to help his work on the drums and cymbals. Man, can he ever pop those suckers.

Rebekah completed her nursing education online and is now an RN to complement her PhD in philosophy. She had planned to write a new book on panentheism, but at the last minute she accepted a State Department assignment working with starving orphans in North Korea (and keeping an eye on "Dear Leader"). We'll sure miss her while she's away.

Following a series of colonic irrigations earlier in the year, Jeff's calm personality became even more serene. He is now studying jazz bagpipes and interpretive dance. The website for this unusual combination is up and running, and Jeff has plans to shoot a documentary film highlighting the cultural possibilities. When he's up late at night, he often goes downstairs with his bagpipes to jam with Cooper.

And so it goes.

HAPPY HOLIDAYS!

A FEW COMPLAINTS, IF I MAY

My lifelong friend is dying of cancer.

We started kindergarten together and have remained good friends.

That's unusual these days.

His cancer is a rare one, creeping up his spine like Boston ivy. He's
> become quite wealthy and has had all the top
> American doctors try to help but they can't seem
> to stop it. Why would you have to die in your
> fifties just when it looks like you've got it made?

Life doesn't always work out the way you plan, I guess.

That's a feeble, distasteful excuse, and if you have a better one please put it

here ⟶ *[*   *]*.

I would have had a big sister but she only lived a few
weeks. Hole in her
       spine called spina bifida. Today they probably
       could have fixed
       it, but not back then.

I always wondered what she would have been like.

And would I be different if she had lived?

What do you say when people ask if you're the oldest?

My aunt lived to be eighty-something and told only
one person, her
       daughter, that she had accidentally killed her
       baby sister
       with tainted milk. My cousin told me.
       She was milking the cow and carelessly let the animal
       kick the bucket over and got barn-floor dirt
       into the milk. She was afraid to tell what
       happened. The baby
       got the milk. Back then they called it *summer*
       complaint. There was no
       antibiotic to stop the unstoppable diarrhea. Now
       we know it as
       E. coli.

My grandmother may have jumped into a swollen river and
       drowned when my mother was nine because she
       found out Granddad
       was sleeping with the maid. Mom was never
       really happy, even when things were going well.

Her mother's untimely and mysterious death
may have had something to do with it. Her mom
might have slipped on the riverbank and fell in,
but people prefer to believe the worst.

Eternity must be a circle. Life is not easy, but there's always
the sun we're circling hiding behind the clouds.
Nothing stays the same. All of us search for
something that's been there all along.

Bring it on.

TO MY CHILDREN, SIX AND FOUR

Damp little bodies, bursting with life to frame
Your unblemished souls and curious eyes
That see like Röntgen's odd device,
You see the blossom, not the slice of fragile life.
Oh do not change, I ask, or die,
Oh do not change or die.

You fit your skin so guilelessly
Yet burn white-hot, but not of pose or spin
But of what's real and true and what is not.
Daddy, why is there grass? You ask and compel my
love entire.
Oh do not change, I beg, or die.
Oh do not change or die.

Do not grow up and try to be
Sophistication's template, or the author
Of some modest deed, which, while adequate for
normal life,
No longer sings of poetry.
Oh do not change, I *pray*, or die.
Oh do not change or die.

A VERY SHORT SHORT STORY

(*CHOKING*)

I blow position from the eight ball to the nine because I'm choking my guts out. Now I'm stuck with a razor-thin cut instead of a gimme. Pocket the nine, I win my first pro tournament and fifty grand. Maggie finally gets a house and doesn't leave me. Miss it, I sell out. She's gone with the baby. I draw down on the nine, make my swing arm feel oily, and stroke the cue ball carrying my ridiculous life.

ICE STORM
(APOLOGY TO ROBERT FROST)

With amoebic passengers riding crystal spaceships,
    the tumbling ice deposited a frozen coating to cosset
    the holiday-hushed streets.

Trees morphed into upside-down chandeliers
    along a slippery, shiny Christmas landscape.
    Impartial ice enshrouded all life
        while gravity defiled senile tree limbs.

Diamond rings (sometimes called "ice") couldn't
sparkle enough to rival
    the blinding reflection of ice over
        Aurora, as the town is called, though no
        borealis,
            ever shone more than the bright
            morning after
                a bittersweet gift from Nature.

Living rooms fell silent as the talking, flickering
>   boxes were struck dumb and dark by snapping
>   wires.

Frozen water annexed all power, ruling absolutely. Without
>   the tele-pablum, Aurorians had to talk or read or
>   even think.

In Quito, Ecuador, there are two little girls, Transito and
Fermina,
>   who have never seen ice.
>>   When they do they will find it much like fire.

TALKING TO STRANGERS

Annie tried to blame having an affair on her daddy's malignancy. That's what she called it—malignancy. It's so like her that she wouldn't utter the c-word and she called him *Daddy*, always.

I turned white as a scar when she confirmed what I already knew. I'd been creeping her personal cell phone, not the one she uses to sell real estate, and the same number kept showing up under "recents." I remembered her gal pals' numbers and this wasn't one of them. I followed her to an after-work bar and saw the two of them go in together. It should have been harder for me to find out. She's not devious enough for that sort of thing.

What was there to say? Nothing came to me. When she got home my suitcase was already in the car. Five more minutes and I'd have been gone.

"Ky, don't go," she kept saying. Her voice trembled. Her face was flushed. Tears made streamlets down both cheeks. "Can you imagine how I feel? Daddy's got malignancy in his lungs, and I'm falling apart. This guy at the office, his wife's got malignancy in her breast, so we talked a lot to try and support each other. It didn't occur to me it could go further and he would push it. I was weak. It only happened twice and I've already told him not to come near me again. I swear it meant nothing. Talk to me. Don't leave."

For half a minute I couldn't make a sound. My mind was blank. Then my face scrunched up all ugly. I said: "I don't buy it. Once? Maybe that's conceivable. Barely. But you went there again." I walked out. I was imagining his hands on her—who did what, with which, to whom. The pain was a palpable, physical thing, like stepping on broken glass. I wanted her to hurt as much as I did.

Although it turned out quite well, Paris was not my first choice. I'd been there before. I wanted to go somewhere I'd never been, someplace alien. But the first available plane with a first-class seat went to Orly, and I needed to move, to feel my body hurtling through space. During the flight with its fine wine and food, I felt drained. I was too bummed out to sleep despite my stretch-out seat/ bed. Eventually I half-napped, just enough to semi-dream. I was listening to Garland, Annie's father, trying to tell me something. But he kept gesturing with a Hanged Man tarot card in his hand, and I couldn't follow him.

I almost didn't, but when I got to the Hotel George V, I texted Annie: "I'm in Paris. I want to be left alone." I slept much of the day and had a quiet evening. The next day I went walking. I don't know who found whom, but

I was wandering at the Pompidou fountains when Ilse spoke to me and I smiled and gestured a hello. Not all who wander are lost, it's said, but I was lost. Centre Pompidou is supposed to be a lighthearted place but it wasn't working for me. My dark thoughts, replayed again and again, had produced uninterrupted melancholy during the flight and since arriving in France.

The fountains make people smile. The unexpected dose of wry, avant-garde wit is effective. Waterspouts twirl and loop. Day-Glo, Dubuffet-inspired whirligigs twist and turn as water splashes them. A bright-blue derby hat bobs in the waves as if being worn by an underwater gentleman. Next to the fountains is a huge building with its insides hanging out. The whole effect makes an irreverent satire against the usual European fountains and buildings with cherubs and gargoyles and spitting fish in their verdigris pomposity. The Centre Pompidou attracts a merry crowd of tourists and overactive children. The locals powerwalk by and try to seem indifferent. The tourist fathers act nonchalant while taking cell-phone pictures to brag about when they get home.

Here's what Ilse said to me: "*Il est étrange que l'on puisse être malheureux ici.*"

"Sorry," I said, looking for the first time into her showstopping face. "I don't speak French."

"I said it is strange that someone could be unhappy here. It must be difficult in a place like this."

"Not really. Right now it's easy for me. You speak wonderful English—without a French accent."

"Ilse," she said, extending her hand. It was thin and feminine but strong. "Ilse von Stomm." The name rolled beautifully the way she said it: *Eeel-zah.* "Originally Austrian from Vienna, but now studying at the École des Beaux-Arts." Her smile revealed perfect teeth just the right white for teeth. I hoped she was dropping the handkerchief.

"I'm Ky, and if you will permit me to say so, Ilse, you're gorgeous. I'm sorry if my depression is so obvious. I'm running away from home, and I've only been in Paris a day. I'm an American."

"Thank you for the compliment. You did not look the happy tourist. I think that's why I spoke to you, which is not something I normally do. Should I be afraid of you? What do you do in America? And why are you alone?"

We sat down on a nearby bench.

I couldn't stop staring. She was still smiling and I thought every soul in the plaza had to be staring at us—or, rather, at her. She defied the predictable color patterns like blonde hair and blue eyes. There were colors, but they were dazzling fusions. Ilse's hair couldn't decide between auburn and blonde and was cropped in a fuzzy burr. Her eyes were gray going on green. It wasn't a trick of contact lenses. Her lips were tumescent, swollen to exactly the same size and veneered with red lipstick the color of sex itself. The bee-stung lips kept her from looking little-girlish. A spackling of light freckles crossed her nose like Shakespeare's flaw that enhances. Her hips and breasts were storybook. My hormones said hey.

"You have nothing to fear from me, and I retired at age thirty-two a year ago from professional baseball. But didn't they teach you growing up in Vienna not to talk to strangers?" I tried to smile my most winning smile. The humid air wafting around the fountains coated her skin, made her glow.

"Of course they did. But I don't always do what I'm told. Do you mind talking? I thought you were American when I saw you, and I like America very much. I'm having my own crisis since my thirtieth birthday is in a week. I addressed you in French in case I was wrong."

"First of all, I certainly don't mind talking," I said. "I think talking to strangers is usually easier than talking to someone you know. You can tell a stranger the unvarnished truth. Sometimes talking to a friend requires nuance, or at least a sugar coating. How did you know I was American?"

"The shoes. It's not that hard. The shoes are different, and there's a certain look."

"You actually like America? That's not fashionable these days, is it?" I checked out my tasseled Cole Haans.

"I suppose not. But for one thing among many, I like that you Americans don't smoke cigarettes anymore. Many Europeans still do. They smoke and pose. It looks so silly to me, like they are more concerned with how they look than what they are. Style over substance. Americans are more direct, and I like that. I'm French-negative but Paris-positive. Besides, I studied in America and loved nearly everything I saw. I also prefer English. It's much more elastic than French or German."

"Ilse, you've taken my mind off my troubles. Thank you. I appreciate it more than you know. I don't want you to think I'm being too forward with a stranger, but the word gorgeous isn't strong enough. I see Marlene Dietrich in your eyes. Did she will them to you?"

"I wish. My eyes did enjoy seeing you smile, in case you're wondering, and when I noticed you I thought of that British actor Jeremy Irons. Handsome but sad. Marlene lived in Paris, you know. I once saw her window-shopping along the Avenue Montaigne. My parents had brought me here for the first time. I was a child, but my parents explained who she was. She'd gotten old, of course, but still had that look. She died here in 1992."

"I think I knew that," I chimed in.

"Where in America do you live? What did you mean about running away? And what about the baseball?" She made it three syllables: *base-a-ball.*

"I live in the Midwest. In St. Louis. A baseball pitcher all through college and eight years in the major leagues. I was lucky to have lasted that long and, of course, it was fantastic to me financially, but most mornings my tenderized shoulder and knotty elbow remind me of the wear and tear. Yesterday I confirmed my wife's been unfaithful, so I had to leave. The first flight with a good seat came to Paris. Nothing good could have happened if I stayed. I had nothing to say to her, absolutely nothing. Now, something good has happened. I'm sitting here talking to you, telling a beautiful stranger my life story.

"Let's not talk any more about it. I'd rather eat and drink. I'm ravenous and parched, and ready for an early dinner. Early by Paris standards. Ilse, *Eeeelza!* Could I please invite you to help me drink an appalling amount of wonderful French wine and wear out a fork? That's the perfect prescription for me right now, and since it's early I'll bet we can slide into a three-star somewhere. Let's throw out all the rules we're usually forced to live by. Let's be two strangers who decide to celebrate something, I don't know what. Life? Tuesday?"

She looked alarmed for a split second, then said: "It's a great way to leave the blues behind but I'm not sure I should do that. I don't know you, and I can't afford to eat out on my art scholarship."

"*Tu ne comprend pas.* You see? I know a little pidgin French. You don't understand. I'm paying for everything. It's my invitation. Please come with me. We'll never know each other unless you do. Look, life is short and death is long, and the best things are spontaneous. Let's break the rules. The cost doesn't matter at all. If I go alone nothing will taste the same, and your English will suffer."

"I hope you know what you're saying about the cost. This is Paris. Are you sure?"

"I'm positive. Let's go for the best. Which way?"

* * *

The maître d' at Restaurant Guy Savoy had waxy skin that suggested delicacy, but he affected the pomp of a powerful mandarin keeping the rabble way from his imperial majesty. He introduced us to our waiter, Hubert (*Oo-behr*) and said he was glad they could seat us after our last-minute call.

Ilse and I giggled at the pomp and circumstance when no one was looking, especially after a fine bottle of Bollinger champagne and a good start on a 1982 Pomerol Bordeaux.

By now, Ilse's initial reluctance to a celebratory dinner with a stranger had vanished. She was happy and we easily called each other Ky and Ilse. What were we celebrating? I wasn't sure but I was happy. Any thoughts of my marital troubles were dissipated by the stunning woman across from me.

Hubert complimented our choices. He spoke accented but adequate restaurant English. He laughed when I told him he probably praised the choices of all his customers. Ilse ordered the initial food and her Franco-Austrian knowledge was evident. I insisted she not look at prices. She started us with *plateau de fruits de mer* to go with the *champagne*, a stunning presentation of raw and cooked shellfish served on ice and seaweed on a tiered silver platter that could have passed for a chandelier. There were lobster tails and claws, oysters, clams, periwinkles, mussels, and prawns plus ambrosial sauces to dredge them in. We devoured a yeasty baguette crust by lovely crust.

With the Bordeaux came braised lamb with canne-llini beans for me and smoked duck with tangerine-rosemary salad for Ilse. Next I ordered a Chambertin Grand Cru Burgundy to accompany Ilse's game course choice—roast, stuffed partridge with sorrel pesto, and minted potatoes. A small dish of rhubarb flecked with the Corsican cheese brocciu cleansed our pallets. Hubert was now in ecstatic agreement with our choices. Ilse translated as he swooned in French. He made exaggerated faces as we discussed first growths. When he left the table I told Ilse he was swelling up like a poisoned pup and blinking his eyes like a toad in a hailstorm. I knew it would test her English. She smiled and awaited clarification.

The food was brilliant, the wine almost magical. We were getting buzzed but in a regal way. The service proceeded seamlessly. The gleaming mahogany and brass of the revered Michelin three-star shone beneath a stained glass skylight. Our legs touched and we didn't move them right away. Something was happening. I told her I felt like we were in a movie, or maybe a magazine ad. We pretended we might throw food. She figured out the toad in a hailstorm and liked it, but she didn't want to think about a poisoned pup.

"Do you have these sayings in Midwest America?" she asked.

"Lots of them. You learn them in small towns, or if you hang around locker rooms."

"I've only been to Chicago plus being a student in New York City. Tell me about a small town. One that's unusual."

"Muscatine, Iowa," I said.

"Tell me about it."

"There's a tire recapping plant, a ketchup factory, and a button museum. People from Mexico come in the summer to pick the mountains of tomatoes that become ketchup."

"What's tire recapping?"

"I like it when you need translation," I said. "For a while I thought your English was better than mine."

I explained about recaps and told her about the dive bar where drinkers pass a seed cap for donations. They give the money to a woman named Dorothea, who takes off her clothes and dances on the bar. She has a wooden leg and only one breast. There's a thin red line where the other breast should be and a dart in the wooden leg so everyone knows it's wood. The men watch, but they aren't rowdy like you might expect. They watch with the same mixture of fascination and expectation shared by fans of boxing and car racing. The leg clatters along, pulled by her hip gyrations but not quite in synch with the jukebox. The missing breast is sad, especially with its former twin bouncing around. Some of the men who've seen the act before hardly look up from their beer. They clap for five seconds when she's finished.

Ilse was confused. Her expressive face was compressed into a sad look and for a moment I thought she might cry. Then the look cleared and she said: "What's a seed cap?"

I made her tell me about growing up in Vienna, Austria. She said it wasn't always romantic, as you might think, and there were still Nazi-types who ought to work in the ketchup factory cleaning the Mexicans' shoes. She spoke of the violin lessons she dreaded each week until she could play Strauss waltzes. That changed her mind completely. She said most of the sophistication prized by residents in the world's beloved cities is shallow pretense and self-congratulation. Ilse varied from moment to moment between toughness, with a masculine edge, to complete femininity. She touched my arm like we'd known each other a long time. The mutual attraction was obvious, at least to me. I thought of Annie and her fling, or whatever it was. I didn't feel the slightest guilt sitting with and being deeply attracted to this lovely stranger half a world away from home.

We were feeling the complete loss of inhibition, a gift from the wines, when I ordered desserts and a half bottle of Château d'Yquem Sauternes, a dessert wine that's heaven in a glass. Ilse said she couldn't eat another bite but when her Grand Marnier soufflé arrived, she did. It only took one sip of the Château d'Yquem with a taste of my mille-feuille to make me close my eyes and take a deep breath of appreciation. The combinations exploded in our heads with a sublime balance of richness. Hubert extolled the cheeses. They looked and smelled fascinating, but by then we really couldn't. We joked about skipping the cheeses because we were starting a new diet. *L'addition* arrived. Ilse peeked and inhaled sharply. I made it a point not to look because I knew it was well into four columns of Euros. I laid out my Platinum card and truly didn't care.

After Hubert cheerfully disappeared with the bill and I was doing mental math to calculate a 25 percent tip to add to the normal service charge, I looked at Ilse and yet again was innocently stricken. I took her delicate hand and gave it a slow, gentle kiss while saying, "Happy thirtieth birthday in a week, dream woman. You might never be more beautiful than you are this moment." She placed the kissed hand behind my neck and drew me close. I didn't resist at all. Who would? She pressed her full lips directly on mine and we kissed so long that when we finally looked up, Hubert was standing nearby and grinning broadly. I have no doubt he took us for man and wife. "*Bonne chance, homme et femme*!" he said with gusto. "Godspeed."

We walked for miles after our unforgettable dining experience, departing the restaurant on the Quai de Conti and ambling along the Seine in no hurry whatsoever until we crossed to the Right Bank over the Pont Neuf and then up the Rue de Rivoli. We talked about the food, of course, and Ilse's sculptures and my years as a big-league pitcher. We crossed back to the Left Bank toward the heart of Saint-Germain-des-Prés. We paid a visit to the famous Brasserie Lipp. Ilse had mineral water while I sipped a large cognac, which was a wonderful mistake. She didn't seem interested in talking about herself but eventually I learned bits and pieces. A brief relationship with a French boyfriend had ended. He posed a lot, she said. She hadn't seen her parents in Vienna for a year, but her relationship with them was fine. She needed to make a trip home. Her professors raved over her sculptures based on pregnant women and entered them in competitions. That produced serious gallery attention and a major first-place award for her pregnant woman with a peacock for a head. "My life isn't that interesting," she said. "Tell me about Annie."

"We met at a classic-movie revival during college. We debated whether popcorn could be flavored or should stick with butter and salt. Our first date was to an old movie, *The Graduate*. We were married in six months. Until recently, when her father got sick and she changed into someone I hardly know, we still watched movies together and went to the local art-movie house to see things like *The Treasure of the Sierra Madre*, *The Quiet Man*, *The Grapes of Wrath*, and weird movies like *Eraserhead*, *La Grand Bouffe*, Fellini stuff."

"I love Fellini," Ilse offered. "The faces, those people, are they real? Where did they come from? What are their lives like?"

"Just four months ago Annie and I went to Ireland for ten days. Everything was still fine between us. Her father's cancer hadn't yet been diagnosed. We drank Guinness in the pubs and sang Irish songs. The misty Irish rain would get Annie's hair damp and matted down, so I told her she looked like a newborn. She said the Irish have such pale skin they look like they've just had surgery."

"Why did you get suspicious of her?"

"One night Annie got up in the middle of the night. She never does that. When she came back to bed I pretended to be asleep and waited until she was asleep again. I got up and found her purse on the closet floor next to the bathroom. I thought I'd heard a zipper and running water when she was up. I opened the purse. The plastic diaphragm case was on top and was still damp where she'd put it away with wet hands. We'd never used a diaphragm. Annie sells real estate and had been out on showings that evening. She came home later than usual and seemed tousled and nervous."

"What did you feel like at that moment?" Ilse asked.

"Like I'd been punched in the gut. I wanted to slap her face while she slept. But, of course, I didn't. There was a chance of some other explanation but I couldn't think of one. I laid there staring at the ceiling in the dark. The next day I started checking her phone.

"I couldn't believe what was happening. My shoulders and neck ached constantly. I kept thinking about the good times, the things we enjoyed together, how all that was over. What had happened? It didn't seem real.

"Then there was the double standard. A few years ago when my baseball team was on the road and Annie stayed home pregnant with Ella, there were temptations. Lots of them. Athletes have groupies just like rock bands. I had a one-night stand with an interesting college girl. I felt bad about it immediately, but the fact is, I did it. There's no denying that. I made it a point not to see the girl again. But I can't compare that to what Annie has done right where we live. I was very careful to make sure she couldn't find out and couldn't be hurt. I don't excuse what I did, but I don't think the two events compare. Am I wrong? Am I using the double standard just to make myself feel better? It just doesn't seem the same."

"I don't know," Ilse said. "I see your point. But if I were Annie it might seem the same to me."

"But that's just it. Annie doesn't know, can't know, will never know. She can't be hurt. On the other hand, I hurt."

"Annie doesn't know, but you do," Ilse said. "By leaving you've made sure she's hurting now. Whether she hurts from what she did or from what you did by leaving her, or both, the emotional pain is the same."

"Maybe. But it doesn't seem the same to me." I shook my head as I thought about it. "Those first few nights, and it's hard to believe it's less than two weeks ago, I'd wake up thinking the most random thoughts about her. How I didn't really know her. How she loved bug zappers. Why would I think of that? Have you ever heard of anyone giving much thought to bug zappers? She thought they were better than TV. Real life and death with spotlights and a soundtrack, she said. And I thought about our daughter, Ella, a grade-schooler who looks just like Annie. Normally they're a cheerful pair to be around. That changed when Annie's father got sick. He's such a vigorous and likeable guy, then out of the blue he's fighting for his life. Garland has a company that helps farmers sell their wheat and soybeans to China. He's done really well. When he got sick Annie acted the same as when she miscarried in her second pregnancy. For two weeks I didn't know her. I'd come home and find her whacked out, teary makeup smeared on her face. Then one day she was better. I thought she had worked her way through it. I thought she was fine. It wasn't long after that when she had her fling."

Ilse said nothing, but looked steadily at me without blinking as we strolled along. There was a long silence. Then we both spoke at once.

"She sounds—"

"Will you please—"

"You first," I said.

"I started to say she sounds like a good person." Ilse paused. "And marriage is supposed to be about more than sex. What did you say to her? Maybe if you told her about your own fling and forgave her and neither of you talked about it again? What were you . . . "

"I was about to say will you please walk with me to my hotel? Or maybe we could taxi or Uber? I suddenly feel intoxicated and tired. Maybe that invitation sounds a little suspicious, but I promise to do only what you wish. If I forgave her—and I see where you're going with that—I'd want her to change real estate offices so she wouldn't be around the guy she slept with. That still makes me feel sick. Surely you understand that?"

* * *

If I'd been seriously trying to seduce Ilse, I would've talked earnestly about circumstances and fate. I would've said that once in a while the normal rules we live by can be suspended, just for an hour or two. I would've told her it's possible for two people to make love, maybe even just once, and keep it a treasured secret forever. I would've said she's a good person, and I'm a good person, and we're both healthy adults with normal urges. So as long as we didn't take the decision lightly, sex for us this night was desirable and forgivable. But I didn't say any of those things. I'm not sure why.

When we got to the Hotel George V in the Avenue George V, what I said was: "Will you come in and stay with me? At least for a while? This place is wonderful. My room should be in a palace."

"Yes," she said calmly. "Yes, I will."

* * *

Her body was as unspeakably beautiful as her face. I trembled as we kissed again and again and I slowly removed her clothing and she removed mine. As we laid down together in the perfectly draped, fairy-tale bed in the storybook room, we touched and explored each other. She felt so lush I didn't know whether to pray or cry or laugh. I saw the fresh flowers next to the bed so I began to cover her naked and perfect breasts and neck and stomach with petals, taking my time and making patterns of intense colors. She was quiet and watched me until the bouquet was used up and the stems stuck out of the crystal vase like string-trimmed grass. I settled down close beside her and put my head on her chest and breathed deeply her bottomless feminine essence, imbued and pollinated with the sweet smell of the petals, until at last I felt an inner peace.

* * *

I awoke. Fabulous alcohol and fabulous calories oozed from my eyeballs and glued them shut. I had no desire to open them anyway because I had no clue where I was. Slowly at first, then in a rush, reality shouldered its way back in, and I knew Ilse was gone and we had not made love beyond our play. It was five in the morning. We had realized just in time that it wasn't the thing to do. Ilse played the leading role in that decision because I couldn't have stopped us alone. Despite my intoxication, which sometimes obliges the male of the species to be willing but unable, I remembered my full arousal and sudden sobriety. Somehow it felt righteous to kiss and say good night, then put her in the pre-paid Uber back to her école. The mystery was still alive.

I washed out my eyes and blinked. This set off a pounding in my head to match the pounding heart in my chest. I was slightly sick and unhappy that this day was beginning. I went back into a light sleep for an hour and didn't move a muscle. Slowly, ever so slowly and despite my effort to hold it at bay, I returned by degrees from that vague and uncertain state where all is dark and caught between life and death. My sleep had been insulted by disturbing dreams caused by the fabulous alcohol. As consciousness again shoved aside the unconscious brain, I was aware of a sadness that moved to the center of me. The sadness was headquartered in my spinning brain but it had opened branches in my heart and stomach. A rattling sigh issued from my dry mouth as I sat up and looked around. Each breath was an effort; there seemed to be little air in the room. I was compressed into the present tense. There was no past and certainly no future.

My emotions rushed together into an intense moment that exploded into a burst of self-pity and sobbing. Tears ran down my cheeks. Someone had climbed inside me and was going mad. Was it possible that this complicated fury, these deep feelings, were part of me? I found the sensations alien. Annie's face appeared. It was so familiar, so comfortable. But I was seeing it for the first time. I knew her, but she was a stranger. The situation couldn't be real. Other marriages crash and burn, but not ours. No way. If I don't grow old with Annie, what's the alternative?

I tried to remember my troubled dreams, nightmares really, as I began to move around. I was swinging on a wire through trees that had faces instead of leaves. I was swimming downstream in a strong river current that was picking up speed. I lurched around the posh room swallowing aspirin for my head and Zantac for my belly. I stood in the glass-and-tile shower with the water too hot and shaved with my eyes closed. I sang "I'm Popeye the Sailor Man" to alter my mood. Eventually I dressed and walked out into the overcast, chilly Paris morning with no idea whatsoever of where I was going or what I was going to do.

* * *

Somewhere between the Anjou pear and the *pain au chocolat* with strong coffee I felt the first inkling I might live through the morning. I had walked the streets, mobile but aimless, for an hour while nibbling the warm croissant and drinking bottled water from a street vendor. I was seated outdoors at Les Deux Magots, alone and glad to be that way. The streets were bustling with college-aged people from the schools nearby in the Saint-Germain-des-Prés area, rushing around on missions that no doubt seemed vitally important to them but probably weren't so much considering the history of the universe. The church of Saint-Germain-des-Prés towered over the anthill of human activity, just as it had for seven hundred years. I knew Ilse was in class not far away since the École des

Beaux-Arts was in the neighborhood. I wanted to look up and see her walking toward me. I was reading through bloodshot eyes hidden by my sunglasses, despite the gray day. An article in the *American Herald Tribune* said Parisian men were no longer routinely keeping mistresses. I've no idea what the day-old *Le Monde* newspaper said (I rescued it from table-leveling duty), but it was pleasantly distracting to browse the pictures and accent-marked headlines to try and extract any meaning.

I had the sensation I was waiting for something. For what I had no idea. Maybe I wanted a thunderclap of clarity to tell me whether my life with Annie was over. If something as important as the love of your life comes to an abrupt end, shouldn't there be a dramatic moment when you know it? Shouldn't the background music swell to a long, deep, sad chord? That's how it works in the movies. That's the trouble with real life. No soundtrack.

I walked again. Through the petite side streets and parks of the oldest section of a glorious city I sauntered without direction. I walked past the beautiful primary building of Ilse's school and knew she was inside. I stopped and felt something primal. What should I do next? A line of ancient philosophy ran through my synapses: "If no one asks me, I know. Yet if I have to explain it to him who asks, I know not."

Vignettes played themselves out in the streets like living theater. A sweet-faced boy in a barber shop was getting his first haircut; a funeral procession exiting a church was led by a thin woman in all black carrying a white flower in her folded hands; a man in his undershirt stood in an open window, taking a pill with drinks of bottled water; two shopkeepers spoke animatedly and took turns touching each other's coat sleeves; in the middle of a quiet street the upper half of a jowly, hard-hatted man stuck out of a manhole, unmoving, the rising smoke from his cigarette the only evidence he wasn't an art installation made of clay.

The hurt inside me began to soften when the day turned soggy. A soft mist enveloped Paris. I kept seeing Annie's face, and Ella's, and even Garland's. My own problems seemed trivial next to his fight to keep living. The important part of losing a marriage, I realized, was losing the day-to-day friendship, the keeping-you-company part. The thought of living without that felt like it would be an amputation. I had a sinking spell and headed back to the hotel and the bed.

* * *

Ilse's note was carefully folded into an envelope and taped to the hotel room door. It was, of course, in English but written in that peculiar European cursive that resists a quick reading.

Hello, Ky. You gave me the most interesting and wonderful afternoon and evening I can remember. You are a sensitive man. Our attraction to each other is strong and feels obvious to me. We did the correct thing in stopping where we did. Now what? I imagine you will need to return to America to see what happens next and I need to make a trip to Vienna to visit my parents. Can we meet at the fountain at noon tomorrow to say good-bye for now? I will be there, blushing at my uninhibited behavior yet wanting to send you off with a kiss.

—Ilse

I read the note three times and felt better with each reading. The maids had cleaned the suite and changed the Frette linens. I snuggled into them and had the best two-hour sleep of my life. When I awoke I felt like a new man.

After a bracing shower and generous use of the George V's extensive and expensive lavations, I dialed Garland's cell. It was the time of day in America that Ella might have been at his house, but she wasn't.

"Ky, I know all about it. Where are you?" Garland said when he heard my voice.

"I texted her I was in Paris but wanted to be left alone. How are you feeling?"

"Crappy. Worse than crappy. But they still say I've got a chance to beat it. My hair's gone, and I'm shot through with chemistry. My baby daughter's been crying for two days, and I can't help her. I could always help her, but now I can barely help myself. She's worried sick."

"I'm sorry this spilled over on you, Garland. I hoped that wouldn't happen. I had to leave. There was no choice."

"I know that, Ky. She told me and she's paying for it. She spaced out, big-time. She was vulnerable and the guy in her office was acting way too much like a guy. Who the hell knows why we do what we do? She already told him to not come near her again. She's physically sick about it."

"Have you seen Ella today? What does she know?"

"Sure, I've seen her. She just left. We told her a little white lie, that you had to leave for a baseball-signing obligation. She doesn't know a thing. Annie braces up when she's around. Ky, please come home and deal with it. I'm not trying to say I know how you feel or any of that BS, but I'm asking you to look it in the eye."

* * *

The next morning the skies over Paris were still cloudy, but my mood was sunny. I made reservations to go home the following day but couldn't wait for noon. I arrived at the Pompidou fifteen minutes early and saw her sitting on a bench reading a book in German. I snuck behind her and kissed the back of her neck above her jacket collar. She startled and said: "*Das musst du sein,* Ky." I sat down beside her and couldn't stop smiling.

"You make German sound like music, lovely one," I said. "Since you were reading in German your brain followed along."

She smiled back. "*Natürlich,*" she teased. "You surprised me, but in a very nice way. I promised myself I would tell you first thing today that I have never in my life behaved the way I did with you. Yet I'm not even sorry."

"You have nothing to be sorry for, Ilse. You were the one who stopped us just in time. It was certainly a memorable evening, wasn't it? I loved every second. And I loved your note." With that I scooched closer to her and pulled her face toward mine. The kiss was soft and long and I didn't want it to end. "I hope you have time for a bite of lunch," I said.

The bistro nearby wasn't yet crowded, and the prix fixe menu highlighting simple roast chicken was delightful. We talked honestly and earnestly about everything, including our new relationship. I told her she was hibiscus and I had become a hummingbird. She was booked to visit her parents in Vienna the following week, when her sculpture classes wouldn't be in session. I told her I was taking her advice and going back home the next day to face my problems and that I had no idea how it would turn out. I told her I was aching to see her that evening and take her to the George V for a proper ravishing. She said she felt the same way but knew it was not the thing to do. We exchanged contact information and continued to talk as if we were already lovers.

"I have an idea I've been thinking about," Ilse said. "Let's set a date six months from today at noon at the fountains again. I will be here for sure, absolutely. If you are here on that day, then we both will know we have some kind of future. If you are not here, then I will know you forgave her and decided to be a good dad. Only one text a week each is allowed and it has to be short and deleted at once. What do you think?"

"I think you are not only beautiful, but one smart Fräulein. What if I can't wait that long to see you?"

She smiled that dazzling smile again. "Any plan can be changed with a short text, but if you give it six months you should know what to do."

* * *

Packed and ready to head to the airport, I overheard a college-aged American debating his French friend in the hotel lobby. "I could never live in a country that did not have a long and glorious past," the French *ami* chided his American pal. "I could never live in a country that didn't have a long and glorious future," the American countered, winning the friendly battle with a grin. My car to the airport arrived.

We rolled through the proud city and then through the suburbs, past the matching buildings, the dense neighborhoods, the parks, the people. I especially watched the people. The driver wasn't talkative, and I could look in silence. I had grown a fresh pair of eyes the past few days. I thought about the fountains in six months. I tried to memorize things so I could replay them at will. Ilse's face was easy. I tried to think what I might say to Annie but nothing that came to mind was constructive.

I tried to be honest with myself, to look at the fact that I hadn't been lily-white in our marriage either. I saw Annie with my new eyes. I thought of the saying that Ginger Rogers did everything Fred Astaire did, only backwards in high heels. I still had trouble seeing her infidelity right where we live and after we'd had a child as being the same as mine on the road with a baseball team years ago. I couldn't get a clear signal to myself as to what I wanted to happen.

How will it be when I get there? I wondered. Should I have a plan or just let it happen? I knew I wouldn't whine or stammer. Should I sulk? Think about revenge? Try to describe how damaged I felt? Be forgiving? Blow up and leave again? Tell her I'd met someone in Paris? I knew that playing a preconceived role would be dishonest. Let whatever happens, happen. Life is rich and complicated and the future is uncertain. There's never an immutable truth; truth might depend on the time of day or the angle of view. What's fact at noon is debatable at four.

I was only sure of one thing. Let her do the talking.

LE MENU DE KY ET ILSE

PLATTER OF FRUITS OF THE SEA

On a silver platter or tiered silver platter, place a layer of shaved ice strewn with seaweed. Arrange the best oysters and clams you can find. Add stone-crab claws, Maine lobster, prawns, mussels, periwinkles, and, finally, mignonette, cocktail sauce, and tarragon mayonnaise to lightly touch the seafood in. Serve with champagne or a good Chablis.

• •

BRAISED LAMB WITH CANNELLINI BEANS

Ingredients:

  1 ½ cups dried small white, white kidney, or cannellini beans

  2 tablespoons extra-virgin olive oil

  6 lamb shanks, each ½ to ¾ pound

  1 yellow onion, finely diced

  1 celery stalk, finely diced

2 large carrots, peeled and finely diced

6 garlic cloves, minced

1 ½ cups dry red wine, such as Côtes-du-Rhône,
Cabernet Sauvignon, or Chianti

1 ½ cups chicken broth

1 ½ cups peeled, seeded, and chopped tomatoes
(fresh or canned)

3 tablespoons tomato paste

1 teaspoon chopped fresh thyme

1 bay leaf

Salt and freshly ground pepper, to taste

1 tablespoon shredded lemon zest

2 tablespoons chopped fresh flat-leaf parsley

Directions:

Pick over the beans and discard any misshapen beans and stones. Rinse the beans, place in a bowl, and add water to cover generously. Let stand for about 3 hours.

Drain the beans and place in a saucepan with water to cover by 2 inches. Place over medium-high heat and bring to a boil. Reduce the heat to low and simmer, uncovered, until nearly tender, 45 to 60 minutes. Drain well.

Meanwhile, in a deep, heavy stockpot over medium heat, warm the olive oil. Add the lamb shanks and brown on all sides, 10 to 12 minutes. Transfer the shanks to a plate. Add the onion, celery, and carrots to the pan and sauté over medium heat, stirring occasionally, until the onion is soft, about 10 minutes. Add the garlic and cook, stirring, for 1 minute. Add the wine, broth, tomatoes, tomato paste, thyme, bay leaf, and lamb shanks. Bring to a boil over high heat. Reduce the heat to low, cover and simmer until the shanks can be easily pierced with a skewer, 1 ½ to 2 hours.

Add the beans, stir well, cover and simmer gently until the lamb begins to fall from the bone and the beans are tender, about 30 minutes more. Season with salt and pepper. Remove the bay leaf and discard.

In a small bowl, stir together the lemon zest and parsley. Transfer the lamb shanks and beans to individual plates and garnish with the lemon zest-parsley mixture. Serve immediately.

• •

SMOKED DUCK WITH TANGERINE-ROSEMARY SALAD

Ingredients:

SMOKED DUCK

1 cup fresh tangerine or orange juice

5 tablespoons light brown sugar

2 tablespoons unsulphured molasses

1 tablespoon kosher salt

1 tablespoon coarsely chopped rosemary

Zest of 2 tangerines or oranges, cut into very thin strips

¼ teaspoon each freshly ground white pepper and black pepper

Four 5- to 6-ounce boneless duck breasts, with skin

½ cup long-grain white rice

¼ cup loose black tea, such as Ceylon

TANGERINE–ROSEMARY SALAD

  ½ cup fresh tangerine or orange juice

  ½ small shallot, finely chopped

  2 tablespoons champagne vinegar

  2 teaspoons honey

  ½ teaspoon minced rosemary

  ¼ cup plus 2 tablespoons extra-virgin olive oil

  Salt and freshly ground pepper

  2 large tangerines or oranges

  4 cups (packed) mixed tender greens, such as Boston
  lettuce and mâche

Directions:

STEP 1

In a shallow glass or ceramic baking dish, combine the
tangerine juice with 3 tablespoons of the brown sugar, the
molasses, kosher salt, rosemary, tangerine zest, and white
and black peppers. Add the duck breasts and turn to coat.
Cover and refrigerate overnight, turning occasionally.

STEP 2

Line a wok and its lid with heavy-duty foil, allowing a 6-inch
overhang around both the wok and lid. Add the rice, tea,
and the remaining 2 tablespoons of brown sugar to the wok
and stir to mix. Set the wok over moderate heat and cook
until wisps of smoke rise up from the smoking mixture.

STEP 3

Pat the duck breasts dry with paper towels and arrange them
on a 9-inch round cake rack. Carefully, set the rack in the wok

over the smoking mixture. Cover with the lid and crimp the foil tightly all around. Smoke the duck breasts over moderate heat for about 18 minutes, or until the meat is medium rare. Transfer the duck to a cutting board and let rest for 5 minutes.

STEP 4

In a blender, combine the tangerine juice, shallot, vinegar, honey, and rosemary. Blend until smooth. With the machine on, gradually drizzle in the olive oil until the dressing is smooth and slightly thickened. Transfer the tangerine dressing to a large bowl and season with salt and pepper. Using a small, sharp knife, peel the tangerines. Cut in between the membranes to release the sections.

STEP 5

Carefully remove the skin from the duck and thinly slice the meat diagonally across the grain. Add the greens to the large bowl and toss with the dressing. Mound the salad on plates and scatter the tangerine sections on top. Arrange the sliced duck alongside the salad and serve.

. . . .

ROAST STUFFED PARTRIDGE WITH SORREL PESTO

Ingredients:

  3 large slices of bread

  2 ½ ounces butter

  2 large partridge

  4 generous ounces of thinly cut, streaky bacon

Directions:

Preheat the oven to 425°F. Cut the crusts off the bread and generously butter each side. Cut each slice in half and arrange in two lines in a baking tray. Season the partridge inside and out with salt and pepper. Mix the stuffing ingredients together and push inside the birds.

Place each bird on top of three slices of bread, and cover with butter and slices of streaky bacon.

Roast for 10 minutes, then remove the bacon, basting the birds with the pan juices (do this with the tray out of the oven and the oven door shut to keep the oven hot). Continue roasting for another 5 minutes before reducing the oven temperature to 350°F.

Roast for another 15 to 20 minutes, then remove from the oven and rest, covered with foil, for at least 10 minutes. This is delicious served with breadcrumbs fried in garlic and butter until they are crisp and toasted.

• •

SORREL PESTO

Ingredients:

2 fat garlic cloves

⅔ cup pumpkin seed kernels, pine nuts, or walnuts

20 sorrel leaves

⅓ cup extra-virgin olive oil

¼ teaspoon coarse salt

½ cup grated Parmigiano-Reggiano cheese

Directions:

Place garlic in food processor; process until minced. Add pumpkin seeds; process until ground. Add sorrel; process. Add olive oil and salt and process until creamy. Stir in cheese. Use as stuffing with partridge, then paint onto individual pieces of the bird.

• •

GRAND MARNIER SOUFFLÉ

Ingredients:

  3 tablespoons granulated sugar
  3 tablespoons all-purpose flour
  Unsalted butter, softened, for greasing
  Crème pâtissière, at room temperature
  2 tablespoons Grand Marnier
  1 tablespoons orange zest
  6 large egg whites, at room temperature
  Powdered sugar, for garnish

Directions:

STEP **1**

Preheat oven to 375°F with oven rack in lower third of oven. Stir together granulated sugar and flour in a small bowl; set aside. Cut a 24x12-inch piece of parchment paper; fold lengthwise 3 times (letter-style). Wrap paper around outside top of a 1-quart soufflé dish to form a collar extending 2 inches above rim; secure tightly with string or tape. Rub inside of soufflé dish and parchment collar with butter. Dust with sugar mixture, shaking out excess. Chill dish at least 15 minutes.

STEP 2

Stir together crème pâtissière, Grand Marnier, and orange zest in a large bowl. Beat egg whites in bowl of a heavy-duty stand mixer on medium speed until glossy and stiff peaks form, about 4 minutes. Whisk about one-third of egg whites into crème pâtissière mixture until well incorporated. Gently fold in remaining egg whites until just incorporated. Pour mixture into prepared dish. Place dish on a rimmed baking sheet, and bake in preheated oven until soufflé is puffed and golden brown, 40 to 45 minutes. Sprinkle with powdered sugar. Serve immediately.

• •

MILLE-FEUILLE PASTRY

Ingredients:

PUFF PASTRY

    2 cups all-purpose flour

    1 teaspoon salt

    1 ¾ cup cold unsalted butter

    ⅔ to 1 cup ice water

    1 teaspoon lemon juice

    Flour, for rolling dough

Pastry Cream

  5 egg yolks

  ⅓ cup + 1 tablespoon sugar (90 ml)

  1 ½ cup whole milk (375 ml)

  3 tablespoons flour (45 ml)

  1 vanilla bean, split in half and scraped

  Pinch salt

Assembly

  Icing sugar, for dusting

  Strawberries, for garnish, optional

Directions for puff pastry:

STEP 1

Combine the flour, salt, and ⅓ cup of the butter in a large bowl. Work flour with hands, breaking up butter into pieces until mixture resembles coarse meal. Make a well in the center and pour in the ⅔ cup ice water and the lemon juice. With a fork, gradually bring the flour into the well and mix until incorporated. If dough seems too dry, add the remaining water.

STEP 2

Knead very gently to make a semi-smooth dough. Pat the dough into a flat, 1-inch thick disc. With a knife, mark an X across the entire width of the dough. Wrap the dough in plastic and refrigerate for at least 2 hours.

STEP 3

In a stand mixer fitted with the paddle attachment, add the remaining butter and beat until softened, about 2 minutes. With your hands, form the butter into a square that is about ⅓ smaller than the dough. Wrap butter in plastic. Refrigerate. Chill until firm.

STEP 4

Remove the dough and butter from the refrigerator. Place the dough on a lightly floured surface. Roll the corners of the dough out to about ¼-inch thick, forming a large X shape, leaving the center of the dough unrolled. Place square of the butter in the middle of the X. Pull the rolled-out corners up over the butter to completely encase the butter in dough.

STEP 5

Roll the dough into a 10x20-inch rectangle. Roll dough to even distribution. Rotate the dough so it is horizontal to you. Do one envelop fold or one half turn. That is, fold the right side into the center, then fold the left side to the center. Now, fold the dough in half. This is a completed full turn. Wrap dough in plastic. Refrigerate for 2 hours.

STEP 6

Repeat the full turn, wrap in plastic, and refrigerate for 2 hours. Do one more full turn and refrigerate for 2 hours. Now the dough is ready to use.

Directions for pastry cream:

STEP 1

In a medium bowl, stir together ⅓ cup milk with flour and salt, and whisk until smooth. Add the yolks and 3 tablespoons sugar and whisk vigorously until mixture is smooth and pale-lemon in color.

STEP 2

In a heavy-bottom saucepan, heat remaining milk with the remaining 3 tablespoons sugar and vanilla scraping over medium heat. Heat until milk just comes to a boil. While stirring the yolk mixture, slowly pour ¼ of the hot milk into the yolk mixture. This will temper the egg yolks so they don't start to scramble. Immediately pour yolk mixture into hot milk in the saucepan. Whisk over medium heat until mixture comes to a boil and thickens. Remove from heat immediately. Cover with plastic wrap to prevent skin from forming. Cool completely.

Directions for assembly:

STEP 1

Cut ⅓ off pastry square. Freeze remaining pastry or save for another use. Roll puff pastry to a very thin rectangle measuring 12x16 inches.

STEP 2

Preheat oven to 425°F.

STEP 3

Line a baking sheet with parchment paper and sprinkle with water. Lay dough on top and poke with fork all over to prevent over-rising. Chill 15 minutes.

STEP 4

Bake until golden brown and very crisp. Cool completely on rack.

STEP 5

Trim pastry so edges of rectangle are straight and even in shape. Divide the rectangle into 3 even strips, each about 4 inches wide.

STEP 6

Evenly divide cooled pastry cream onto two strips of puff pastry. Spread evenly. Lay one strip, covered with cream on top of first, lining up evenly. Top with final strip of puff pastry. Dust with icing sugar. Chill for 1 hour before serving.

STEP 7

To serve, cut with serrated edge knife using sawing motion. Garnish each with half of strawberry.

FAKE-NEWS CHRISTMAS LETTER #4

Beloved Friends,

As you know, our annual Christmas letter is sent only to close friends we believe will understand our need to share. We haven't been shy in previous letters about strutting a bit, walking the walk—OK, let's call it what it is—bragging about our accomplishments when we were on top. So it may come as a surprise for you to receive our letter this year, given the newspaper's police reports and vicious rumors that we know all too well. But it's not in our DNA to cut and run when things don't go so well, when things get a little messy. Although it would be easy to skip this year's letter we choose to be honest. Tell it all. Fess up. We continue to share and hope you'll understand. That's the spirit of the season.

The problems this year began with Jeff's failed drug test. He was in Atlanta attending a get-rich seminar on multilevel marketing. The police there claim they'd never seen marijuana stems actually floating in urine. He was befriended, or could we say "turned on," by two of the seminar presenters, Lorry King and Evander Holywine. He met them in a Q & A session after their presentation, and they somehow got him to participate in an experiment using a Rolls-Royce muffler as a bong. Jeff is fairly sure nothing happened between him and Lorry, but his memory is cloudy. He has promised no more contact with Lor and Vander, so Rebekah has taken him back. The only remaining problems from Jeff's time as a pothead, which must have permanently affected his brain, are his urge to adopt kittens (our milk bills are way up) and the mild facial tic. His hands shake a little and there is a burn scar on his chin, but he's trying to make it up to the family. He's working the night shift at a pipe-welding plant and studying a book on ventriloquism with an eye toward show biz.

Rebekah has tried to take it all in stride. She's doing well except for insisting a TV be turned on in every room. She shuffles around the house in her robe staring at the Cartoon Network and sipping Southern

Comfort. We know the sweet whiskey isn't good for her cognition or her figure early in the day like that, and when she hurled up an intact muffin the other day, she promised to cut back.

Savannah's shenanigans haven't helped any this year. She's six now and has learned to use the landline and cell phones. The calls to Afghanistan were what drew the attention of the C.I.A. The worst problem, though, is her answering the random sales calls. Eleven in one day, and she can't say no to anyone. We have a large closet filled with appliances, magazines, various gadgets, and what-not, that we have no use for whatsoever. The collection agencies are persistent.

It was an accident so it's not Cooper's fault he fell down the stairs and now thinks he's a dog. That kind of thing can happen to an active four-year-old. The problems come when he's woof-woofing around the house and bites Jeff's feeding tube. As an "older" father of young children, Jeff has decided against having more kids and has had himself spayed.

To end on a positive note, let us describe our new business venture. Jeff met two other people at the Atlanta seminar. One is called Bullets and the other goes by Six-Pack. We don't think nicknames are any reason not to trust folks. We're all in with them on an ambitious pyramid—ah, make that multilevel marketing—deal involving gold dental crowns and burial plots. We'll be in touch with you about this opportunity.

It's not to be for us this year, but we hope you have the

BEST CHRISTMAS EVER.

FUNCTIONS

Mornings they arise slowly, gently from the sheltering bed

        they tried to rest within.

The insulted knee creaks.

        A fickle foot complains.

An aggravated ligament fires its huffy warning to the brain.

Here is the stuff of poetry. The clock's pitiless tick and march.

The functions and embarrassments to be endured.

Flaking skin is flooded away

        as they clear their curdled throats to speak

        to the aging reflections.

A brittle voice, an eggshell voice thin as parchment
says, predictably:

"Morning."

Teeth are brushed, wind broken, mouthwash gargled.

Where are the books, the music, the paintings

to celebrate our ridiculous, private selves?

AUTUMN

Sometimes I don't have inspired ideas for making
poetry from life.

All I heard in my fancy car was the obnoxious hum of
       the engine, and growls of
        the jammed cars surrounding me, blocking me
        from getting where I wanted
            to be.

Noisy. Mundane. Unpoetic.

The cacophony of jammed cars and depressing radio
news and strong wind

rocking the car was aggravating, burrowing holes in
           my selfish mind.

It wasn't simply wind and noise, it was Armaggedon,
or (*wait for it*),
        The Rapture.

No, not really. It was simply more of the daily
nuisances building that wall to impede my hurried life.

I looked out the window to my right. There in the
blowing leaves
      were two college boys, eagerly playing some
      gusto game
         with beanbag and target.

Imagine that. There was a world outside mine, another
way to see if
      I could only sense it or,
         hear it.

I found my soul and opened it. I could see and hear
the leaves rustling on the pavement and the muffled
voices of the excited boys. The car's motion was not
random but compelled by the lovely, stout wind. I
knew there was more than me, and more than where I
was going. I could smell and feel the
      sensation we call
      autumn.

LETTER TO DAPHNE

Dear Daphne,

I know you will find it weird that I'm writing and mailing this letter to you, since we live only two blocks apart and visit at least twice a week. But I have to tell someone about what has happened. With a friend like you, I'm afraid if I try to talk about it I'll start bawling and howling like a baby. So I'm getting my thoughts down on paper and sending you this letter. You're my bestie, for sure. I'll never be able to repay you for getting those boys in our high school to stop making fun of my name, Denise, as they did by calling me "De-nephew." Maybe in a few months we can talk normally about what's happened. So here goes.

You of all people know how close I am to our twin white labradoodles, Biscuits and Waffles. I say twins even though they aren't related because they look so much alike and the breeder told me they're close to the same age. Ray even gets them mixed up at times and I have to tell him again to look for the freckle on Biscuits' nose. Ray also reminds me that they're both girls and that the breakfasty names seem boyish to him. He's just not as close to my darlings as I am. They love their names. They come whenever I call them, both running to me and climbing up on me to get their little treat cookies that smell like peanut butter. I like to give them both a kiss on the wet nose and then pop the cookie in. They never get tired of it.

Anyway, Ray and I both noticed the slug trails in our back pantry. You know that little pantry room that hangs off the back of our house? We'd find disgusting snotty trails in there some mornings and we couldn't figure out how the slugs were getting in. At least they hadn't figured out how to get into my hand-canned persimmons. That's one good thing. It wasn't Ray's fault that he bought the small packs of snail and slug poison on the internet and forgot to tell me he put a couple of them on the pantry floor. I didn't need to know. But it turns out that stuff is deadly to dogs and, wouldn't you know it, they put something in there to draw the snails and slugs, and whatever it is smells kind of like peanut butter. Biscuits and Waffles were outside in their pen which leads to the back door, just where we usually leave them, but they pushed open the back door and set off the alarm system. They were trying to get at what they thought were their cookies, evidently. They tore the packs open and ate some. We were out to dinner. When we got home the red lights were flashing from the police cars and the neighbors were out in their yards to see what was going on. The four policemen had their guns drawn. They asked us for the front door key so they could check inside and we gave it to them. When they opened the door, Biscuits and Waffles ran outside and had convulsions and tremors while squirting doggy-doo all over the yard. (Yes, it was inside too.) The police figured out that the dogs had tripped the alarm so they left, I must say, in a hurry.

We got the dogs to the emergency vet and they did everything they could, but by the next morning the dogs were worse. Ray and I got no sleep at all. We took them into the city to the Trump Animal Hospital and the expert vets in the critical care unit said they had a fifty-fifty chance of surviving another twenty-four hours. Those great doctors put both of my babies on ventilators and saved them. They survived. I cannot express strongly enough our gratitude to these wonderful women veterinarians who are dedicated to critical care for pets.

I had to look this up, hon, but this poison is called metaldehyde toxicity and it's more common than you think. After ingestion the metaldehyde is converted to acetaldehyde and that stuff is potent poison. It causes tremors, lack of coordination (ataxia), seizures, high temperatures, blood clotting disorder, organ failure and death. What I'm saying, dear Daphne, is don't let your beloved Norwegian Lundehund, Magnus, or your two cats, Edna and Maude, ever get near snail and slug poison if you ever have to use it.

It took more than a week but Biscuits and Waffles are back to their normal loving selves. It's odd that their beautiful white coats have changed color and are now gray (come to think of it, a lot like Ray's hair), but at least they are alive and seem well. Their normal hearty barks at the squirrels in our yard sound a little hoarse and they won't touch the peanut butter cookies I used to give them, but all in all, it could have been much worse.

Love,
Denise

P.S. I'm knitting them new white sweaters so they'll look more like they used to, and I'm putting a snail on one and a slug on the other.

DEAR ME/DEAR YOU

The highway patrol called me at home. It was 10:12 p.m.

(You think you own your own life, but you don't. Dreadful things can happen with no warning; unwelcome news may come from a simple phone call.)

"This is Sergeant Slater. I'm calling for John Browning." His tone was sympathetic but straightforward.

(What he told me didn't seem real. You don't ever anticipate such a phone call. I remember my physical reaction especially. My hands began to shake. My voice trembled as I tried to coax more information out of him.)

"Your parents were driving home from senior night at the country club. The teenagers who slid into them were drinking, speeding, and on the wrong side of the road. Both your mom and your dad are seriously injured and undergoing treatment right now. I wish I could tell you more, but that's all I know."

(I'm an only child. My folks doted on me in my youth. I never got along that well with either of them, mostly because

as a kid I was a know-it-all smartass. I moved to the city ten years ago when I was thirty, and they got a lot smarter. We've been close since then. I visit them often.)

Slater said, "Mister Browning. Please try to be calm. Can I tell the hospital that someone from the family is on the way?"

I told him yes, that I would leave in five minutes and be there in two hours or less. He gave me the hospital's phone number.

"John," the trooper said, brimming with sincerity, "you can't help them if you're in an accident on the way. We've seen this happen before. Please drive carefully."

(I wasn't in the mood for a lecture, but I told him thanks and asked him to please tell the nurses to call my cell number if there were any drastic changes. Cell phones in those days were bulky and unreliable, but our company gave one to every salesman. I felt like I was back in combat in Vietnam with adrenaline flowing through my entire body. You don't know how you'll react until it happens.)

The drive seemed longer than ever. There was a beginning but no end. I tapped my watch, like someone watching a bad movie. The talking heads on the radio were underwater. I had dialed my son and my daughter before firing up my 1992 Chevy Camaro with the "25th Anniversary" badge on the dash. Both of my kids lived far away in large cities but kept in touch with their grandparents. I told them I'd call again when I knew more.

The only interruption from anxiety and boredom was the trucker I heard on my CB monitor. As he passed a young woman, he announced to the other truckers and to me: "Why, honey, I'd crawl a mile on my belly through barbed wire and broken glass just to smell the tires on the laundry truck that picks up your underwear." Despite being unmistakably crude, the rude joke brandished a colorful hock-and-spit twang.

(Don't get me wrong. I'm not admiring some vulgar trucker. I'm just saying under the circumstances it took my mind off my parents for a minute.)

At the hospital I found Mom in critical condition and Dad dazed, asleep, and bleeding from a gash in his head.

(Dear God, I'd really appreciate it if you'd see to it that they come out of this OK. They're not that old, and I've still got some making up to do from when I was a smartass kid. I promise I'll be a better person if you will.)

The nurse said Dad was in shock from his injuries. She said everything possible was being done for Mom. She was out of surgery now and the rest was up to her. In the quiet ominous hours of that difficult night I might have slept for a half hour. The rest of the time I squirmed in the cot they set up for me next to Dad's bed. I listened to his soft moans.

(Maybe I slept more than I thought, if you can call it sleep. I remember a dream where someone was in the room watching both of us. I was yelling at this tall figure in a striped suit surrounded by faint light, "Hey, who the hell are you? What are you doing in here?" And I was hearing an answer that sounded like static: "I've been called a lot of things, John. The one I like best is Beelzebub. I'm always around at times like this to see if I have new recruits. Watch this." Then his tie burst into flames, and he was gone.)

In the morning Mom's vital signs were slightly improved and Dad was sitting up in bed trying to talk and not moan. He asked me to go to their house and bring the letters. He told me where they were. I knew what he was talking about.

My last visit had been three months earlier. By chance, in a garage storage box I found a letter my father wrote to himself in 1939 when he was seventeen. His English teacher had asked his class to write to themselves about their lives and the world in general and then put the letter away to be read forty or fifty years later. Of course, he forgot all about it until I fished it out of the box. Dad sat down immediately and wrote an answer to himself from the perspective of five decades later. The experience delighted him and he wanted to go over the letters again in the hospital, maybe to help push his mind away from Mom's condition. In his room when I returned, after the doctors and nurses cleared out and gave us hopeful news about Mom, he asked me to read aloud.

(I'll admit there were tears in my eyes and a lump in my throat as I began to read.)

Here are the letters exactly as my father, Edward "Biscuits" Browning, wrote them:

March 24, 1939

Dear Me,

Mother is making chicken and dumplings tonight. I'm looking forward to that because since I was seven and the Depression began, so many of our suppers have been beans and corn bread that anything else is a treat. Corn bread is pretty good with Mother's fresh-

churned butter and honey from our hive, however.

    I came from school through the back door into the kitchen, which allowed Mother to show me the chicken in the pot. The first thing she said was, "Can you believe in two months you'll be a high school graduate?" She explained that someone paid Father with a chicken for several hours of tool-sharpening work. Father sharpens tools on the side, as you will remember some day. At first I thought I was in for the "horrors of the Depression" speech with the stirring footnote of how lucky we are to have a chicken. This is what Mother and Father talk about most of the time, laced with their fluctuating opinions of President Roosevelt. When I was younger, I listened. Now I have to leave the room because it's so tedious.

    Writing a letter to myself seems a queer thing to do but Mr. Holmes says I'm a good writer, and a letter is good practice. Remember Mr. Holmes? He says since he's now in his forties he finds it hard to remember what it was like to be a teenager. He wishes he'd written to himself just to be able to read it years later. He also says he will give extra credit.

(Dad was always a good writer. I remember him writing letters to the editor of our newspaper and letters to me when I was in the army. They were always interesting and funny.)

    The idea is to put this letter away and read it a long time from now, say when I'm sixty or seventy years old. Good grief, for the life of me I can't even imagine being twenty-five, much less sixty or seventy. The truth is, I don't know what to say about being seventeen. What am I supposed to compare it to? I guess I should just write whatever.

Should I feel bad about thinking Mother and Father are boring? I don't. I should be truthful, right? I love them, of course, and at times they sense how I feel and give each other looks like they have a secret. But I can't help it. Everything they say and do is predictable. Everything has to fit into their boxes. They don't really listen if I try to offer an opinion or say what I think. They demand respect, but don't give any in return. Mother and Father want to talk about things happening here in our little town, or what the newspaper says about the Depression. Maybe a little about Roosevelt. That's it. I'm not saying we're smarter than the adults or anything, but at school we talk about Hitler and the Nazis, or cars, or girls, or sports. Yesterday we tried to imagine the United States with a dictator—who it would be and what that would be like. At least there's some variety.

Speaking of cars, I just saw the new 1939 Nash Ambassador convertible in a powder blue. Dub Thurman, the guy who owns the biggest grocery store in town and who seems not to have noticed the Depression, bought one and drives through Vern's Burger Bar when his store closes. I hate to admit it, but all of us look forward to Dub's drive-through. He waves at us like the Queen of

England. There's not much more they can do to improve cars. The Ambassador comes in several colors and is really fast. I wish I had the thousand dollars it takes to buy one. I'd take perfect care of it and keep it forever.

Patty Buehler, who I thought was my girlfriend since she asked for my class ring to wear on a chain around her neck, had a party in her parent's basement on Saturday. I got there a little late since I was sacking groceries at Dub's, and she didn't see me come in. She was dancing with Hogie Dunning to the Mills Brothers song "Paper Doll." That was OK, but when the song ended she leaned up and kissed him on the lips. I felt like someone squeezed the air out of me. When she looked up, finally, and saw me she started toward me but I gave her the evil-eye, double-whammy sign like the guy in the Li'l Abner comic strip and then I quickly left the party. That's the end of that. I'll get my class ring back.

(I had a similar experience when I was sixteen, but I didn't know about Dad's until the letter to himself. If you thought about it for a while, you might remember some heartbreaking experience like that from high school. You and I both know what goes on at that age.)

Baseball practice was called off today because of a muddy field from last night's rain, so a bunch of us walked around town after school. When we passed the Cockatoo Tavern Eddie Samsel opened the front door and shouted: "Daddy, come home!" The big guy who owns the beer joint came running out and chased us down the alley, but he gave up after a block and wheezed back to his tavern. A minute later the town's police cruiser drove by and we took off running for no reason at all. The policeman chased us in his car until we stopped. We were in front of the house with the three-legged dog everybody calls Tripod. I don't think that's his real name. The dog was in the yard barking like crazy. "What's going on here?" the cop shouted. "What are you boys doing?" Eddie said, "Nothing, sir. Not a thing. We were just getting some exercise." The policeman shot us a stern look, but he knew he'd been had. "You boys better get on home," he shouted as he drove away. "What's a penny made out of?" someone asked when he was gone. "Dirty copper," the others answered with a smirk.

Harvey Shane told us he read in Time magazine that the Germans are starting to murder Jews. The story said the Nazis forced sixty-two prosperous Jewish people to run through a gauntlet at someplace called Sachsenhausen while Hitler's black-uniformed police clubbed and whipped them. When it was over, twelve of them lay dead with their skulls smashed and the others were mostly unconscious. Eyes were knocked out and faces caved in by the storm troopers. It's hard to believe human beings could do that to other human beings. People around here say America will never get into another European war if there is one. But if the Germans are doing things like that, I have to wonder. Can't anyone stop them?

I came up with an idea. I told the guys we should go door to door and collect little things that say "Made in Germany" on them. Many houses would have some little trinket to donate. We would take these items and make a pile of them on the town square and burn the pile. If towns across the country did this maybe the news would get back to Germany and send a message. Maybe the English and French would join in, who knows? My pals thought it was a bully idea, but we probably won't get around to it. The adults would tell us we shouldn't. They wouldn't like admitting a teenager had a good idea. Like when I told Father my idea for a self-making bed, one where the covers would be hooked to springs so when you pulled a handle the bed would be made. He laughed and said God gave us hands to make the bed and besides, who would have money for such a thing, with the Depression and all?

Now that my class ring is back on my finger and I'm kaput with the deceitful Patty Buehler, I've got a date Friday night with one of our band's majorettes, Gayle Powell. I'm excited about it, but I wouldn't want her to know. Father says I can have the old Plymouth "for a little while." He knows I can drive it as well as he can, but he'll probably ask me to have it back by eleven o'clock. I hope to have enough in my savings within a couple of months to buy a used car for myself.

Several of us are getting together Friday night to play Vox Pop, the new home version of the famous radio program where you answer all kinds of questions. I think I'll be good at it, so I spent the fifty cents the game costs. I hope it's worth it. I have to remember not to be cocky. I doubt if Gayle would like that. She's really good looking and recently broke up with the boy she's been going with since our freshman year. I guess she must think I look OK, but I wish I weren't so tall and had more meat on my bones. Jerry Cossman said I was "Lincolnesque" and called me Abe for a while. My black hair is OK when I can get Mother not to cut it too short. Thank goodness she let me return those denim overalls she wanted me to wear to school, so I didn't have to look like I just fell off the hay baler. Hey, I was just thinking I should ask everyone at the Vox party, even the girls, what they think they would do if there turns out to be a new war with Germany. What would it be like to be shot at? Horrible, I imagine. I hope I never find out. Father never talks about his war days in the summer of 1918 when he arrived on the western front with millions of other American soldiers, but he keeps his old uniform and doughboy helmet in his closet, so he must think about it sometimes.

(Ironic to me when Dad talks about not wanting to know how it feels to be shot at. You'll know what I mean when you read his reply to himself.)

The guys on the baseball team have been calling me "Biscuits." It's true that I could eat a bowl of biscuits with a bucket of gravy, but the nickname came about another way. In the locker room there are plenty of testicle jokes with references to bulls, geldings, mountain oysters, that sort of thing. I was in the shower when Rod Higgenbotham said: "Look at him, boys. The guy's got balls the size of buttermilk biscuits." Rod called me "Buttermilk" at first but then switched to "Biscuits." Now it looks like the name may stick since everybody's using it. But very few people know the origin.

Does the name Addie Lee Vernon ring a bell? She's the little girl about three or four years old who lives down the street. She's the kid sister of Slobbo Vernon. Slobbo is in my class, but no one really knows him. I don't even know his actual first name. He's an odd character, retarded I think, with a dull cast in one eye. The teachers do their best to push him through school. He was caught a couple of months ago trapping birds and burning them at the stake. Slobbo shot Addie Lee in the eye with a BB gun Christmas Day. They say it was an accident. She lost the eye, and immediately became so frightened she stopped talking. Doesn't make a sound. Doc Morrison says it might be permanent. Mrs. Vernon keeps her in the house all the time now. Everyone is buzzing about the situation. "The poor little thing," people say, "what will become of her in that family."

Gerald Turnipseed has become the town comedian with his sense of humor and a new joke every day. He's the only guy who's way taller than me, and he has the gas station across from the courthouse. Here's his latest:

YOU: Gerald, how's the weather up there?

GERALD: There's a telephone in my rear, why don't you call up and find out?

YOU: How you doing, Gerald?

GERALD: No good. I lost a bunch of money this week.

YOU: How is that?

GERALD: Price of bacon went up again, and I ain't got a pig to my name.

YOU: What's the matter, Gerald?

GERALD: Aww. Saturday night's coming up again. I got to go out and get drunk, and I just dread it so.

Well, old boy, this has been fun but that chicken is smelling pretty good, so it's time to move along. I'll give this letter to my teacher, Mr. Holmes, and then put it away somewhere. When you get old you can read it. I still can't imagine being old, but as the saying goes, it's bound to be better than the alternative.

Sincerely,
Me

* * *

June 21, 1994

Dear You,

I can't believe I forgot all about the 1939 letter. Now I can't believe it's been found. Your son found it, actually. (Yes, you have an only child, a son.) He was knocking down a mud dauber's nest in the storage shed and kicked over an ancient cardboard box. The letter was stuck inside a Big Chief school tablet. I must have moved that box many times over the years without ever looking inside. Glad it didn't get thrown out.

Let's start with Addie Lee Vernon. When you wrote about her in your letter, I remember you didn't actually believe she'd never speak again. She didn't. Her mother kept her hidden away in the house. The story was that her mom would sneak up to Addie's room at night, and the girl would be spewing a stream of gibberish in her sleep. But when she was conscious, she was mum after the BB blinded her eye. The school psychologist said the night mumbles were hysterical fear dreams, where the dreamer never knows how the dream turns out and the fear is so overwhelming it stifles normal speech and behavior. Her brother, Slobbo, moved away after being in jail for a while and disappeared.

When Addie Lee was about sixteen she silently bore an illegitimate daughter. The father was never known. The perky little girl was called Lulu and there was never a more devoted mother than Addie Lee. They didn't talk aloud but they had a set of signs and signals that got them along fine. They spent most of their time happily playing together. Addie's mother left them alone. Addie was oblivious to her own appearance but she kept Lulu clean and pretty. The child must have been about five years old when she took a fall and skinned her knee badly. Addie Lee called on all her courage and took Lulu to see Doc Davis. Cowering in fear and teary-eyed, she made signs for the doctor to fix the knee. He swabbed it with iodine, which had to sting like crazy, but Lulu didn't move or make a sound. He covered it with gauze and tape and the two left his office doing well. Shortly after this incident the two were separated for the first time. The state stepped in (I'll bet Doc Davis called them) and had them both examined. Addie Lee had lived in hysteria for so long she was basically unable to speak except in squeaks. Lulu was completely normal, except she had little exposure to spoken words, maybe only to radio. She was alert and interested in everything. With help from a state speech therapist, Lulu quickly learned to understand speech and talk to others. She began school only slightly behind and quickly caught up. Eventually she became a beloved elementary school teacher and remained close to Addie Lee. They lived together until Addie died in her late forties, about a year after Lulu's new husband moved in with them.

The '39 Nash Ambassador is as fresh a memory to me as yesterday. Hey, you, don't we wish you could have bought it then for a thousand dollars and kept it like new. Maybe driving it two, three hundred miles a year? I've checked, and it would be worth forty or fifty thousand dollars in mint condition today, maybe more. I'd probably keep it though. In another few years it might be worth double that to a rich car collector.

Your letter at age seventeen was perceptive in many ways, especially with regard to the coming war. Less than six months after you wrote it, Hitler invaded Poland. England and France declared war on Germany. Later, in a big mistake, Der Führer declared war on America. The draft registration law came in 1940 when you were eighteen, too young. Then the draft began in earnest in 1941 after Pearl Harbor, when you were nineteen, almost twenty. You lied about your age because twenty-one was the youngest age to be drafted, but if you volunteered, the military didn't check it—especially if you were a strapping lad of twenty who easily looked twenty-one. You served in the navy and saw plenty of combat. The Pacific war against the Japs was mostly fought island to island by Marines, but you got quite a taste of it in October 1944 at the Battle of Leyte Gulf, when a kamikaze plane hit your battleship with a glancing blow that strewed shrapnel everywhere. A piece hit you in the thumb, which bled like crazy, and your petty officer put you in for the Purple Heart, over your objection. That medal is in your dresser drawer. You don't need to look at it to remember every detail. That day is as fresh in your mind as yesterday. In fact, every day of your service in the war is like that. You've always preferred to just leave the subject alone, even when your son wanted you to talk about it.

So much that you wrote about couldn't have been foreseen. Small things, like how much cars could improve. Big things, sweeping changes that would happen in the space of a single lifetime, things that would change everything in the world: computers, central air conditioning, antibiotics, satellites, routine air travel.

Then there are things you can't believe have stayed the same or gotten worse: poverty, racism, drug use, alcoholism, convoluted and counterproductive politics. Perhaps the most unexpected change was in you yourself. It wasn't easy after the war, but eventually you learned that nothing counts more than matters of the heart. Love abides. The best path in life is hardly ever clear-cut and mostly messy, but if you get love right you'll be OK.

You were fully mature after your war experiences, though barely twenty-four years old. Your parents were smarter and not boring at all. You began to understand their points of view and see what they'd sacrificed to raise you. Your relationship with them was solid; they were good people. They lived to see your son go through the same process you plowed when you were seventeen, the business of breaking away. This was an excellent reward for Mother and Father. They got to watch you experience their previous dance in the ongoing waltz of new generations. They got to tease you about it and remind you that your son was exactly like you. Pray this dance endures.

Mr. Holmes came through with the extra credit he promised for writing a letter to yourself. You got the best grade in his English class. He told the class your letter was top-notch. You were afraid he was going to read it to the class, but he knew it was too personal for that. He said he could read the spaces as well as the words and that he was looking for the ability of youth to spot hypocrisy, which he found in what was said and also unsaid.

You were correct about your notion of a bonfire of "Made in Germany" items. It didn't happen, although you continued to talk about it. Too bad. It wouldn't have changed a thing but it would have made a folksy, small-town backstory into a footnote to history.

The date with Gayle the majorette turned out fine. She was pretty and smelled good. Your hormones were working overtime. The Vox Pop game didn't last too long because the questions were hard, and only you and one other girl could come up with answers. No one kept score. A lot of Vox Pop survives today in the TV game shows. There was pop music on somebody's record player and you danced and the lights were low so there was some slightly clumsy kissing between you and Gayle. You became quite the item until graduation and then for some time after. You wonder where she is today. You really loved that Glenn Miller Orchestra with "Moonlight Serenade," and you still do. Judy Garland singing "Over the Rainbow" was also hard to beat, and still is.

Your idea of a self-making bed is still waiting to be invented. With today's microcomputers you'd think that could be accomplished. Maybe a tiny wire in the sheets and covers and you push a button and they square themselves away.

Your best friend from high school, Ted, enlisted in the marines the same day you snuck into the navy. Ted was actually twenty-one by then, which made him legal. He was posted to the First Marine Division. They made the first amphibious landing of the war, on Guadalcanal. He was killed by Jap machine-gun fire before he could get off the beach. You still go by and visit his grave at least once a month.

You were part of a machine-gun crew on your destroyer. You knew well the feeling, the fear, of being shot at, mostly by Jap planes, and the numbing fear of death's proximity in war. You dealt with it because you had no choice. Like most warriors, you adopted the fatalistic view that unless it's your time, unless a bullet has your name on it, you won't be hit. And there's nothing to be done about it.

You learned that nobody can tell who will be brave under fire until the time comes. You saw a swaggering deer hunter from Texas frozen with fear while a bookish kid from Boston, a medic, crawled across the ship's deck with incoming fire all around so he could give aid to a wounded sailor. Your life was saved by the courage of a young Cherokee Indian boy from Miami, Oklahoma, who sprinted across the deck to warn you of a Jap plane coming in from behind. You swiveled your machine gun around just in time for the shield to catch five bullets and save the both of you.

You learned that the story from Sachsenhausen Concentration Camp was true, but was only the tip of the iceberg, as the full horror of the Holocaust became known.

After the war you returned to your hometown in southern Missouri. You were the star pitcher on the town baseball team, which played schedules against other town teams in the state. They still called you "Biscuits." Your Lincolnesque body proved useful at providing leverage to throw a baseball. Skinny even became stylish in the 1960s, but by then you had thickened. You can't win.

You worked among the Cherokees in Oklahoma and learned their language while you went to a nearby college and got a teaching degree for English. Mr. Holmes was proud of you. You taught at the University of Missouri and wrote academic papers about Cherokee poetry and culture. Your best-known paper involved another tribe, however, the Creeks. You shined a light on the Creek oral tradition of the chief who loved his language too much. A French missionary came to a Creek village in the mid-1700s, full of self-righteousness but without a translator. The Creek chief thought French sounded barbaric compared to the Creeks' melodious language, so he concluded the man was a demon. The chief prayed to his god for guidance, then ordered his warriors to cut out the arrogant missionary's tongue and burn him alive, which they did.

Native Americans also figured into your crowning social accomplishment. Working with a Cherokee named Yellow Bird Six, you set up a Head Start program for Indian children in northeast Oklahoma, which welcomed all tribes. The benefit of that program continues today. But no accomplishment in your life, my boy, topped your success with your wife, Victoria, and John, your son.

You met Victoria in the parking lot after you pitched a one-hitter in an evening baseball game. She looked at you with her sparkling eyes, and you were toast. You asked her out for a glass of wine and never looked back. She absolutely did not call you Biscuits, ever, though she'd heard the nickname and, much later on, the origin story. You were Edward from the beginning and even today. You loved her, then and now. When your son was a toddler and some of your *baseball pals tried to call him Little Biscuits, she let it be known that she preferred John. You sometimes called her Vic but most often, Victoria. She had a stubborn streak, sure, and there were bumps in the road as with any marriage. But the two of you were so much alike there was always fun in the air.*

Now that you look back on it all, a rush of emotions pushes and pulls you in different directions. It's a carnival. One moment you're soaring in the Ferris wheel with a lovely view of the world below, and the next moment you're being whipsawed by the Tilt-A-Whirl. You swallow the lump in your throat and whisper, "Thanks." You know there's nothing you can change—but if you could, you'd have recognized that an obstacle is not a barricade, that there's a difference between an inconvenience and a serious problem. Like most people, you spent too much time sweating the small stuff. You didn't always remember that when things weren't going well, you were being presented with an opportunity to excel.

Mr. Holmes was on the button. Finding the old letter to yourself and now answering it has proven fascinating. You've been lucky. Optimism about the future is central to quality of life, for sure. Optimism about the past is a bonus, a gift to be savored. Try to keep that in mind for as long as you live.

Sincerely,
Me

* * *

The lead doctor took me aside earlier today and said, "John, you can take your dad home tomorrow but your mother is still touch and go. We think she'll recover, but we can't promise that. Your dad needs to stay in bed a few days. Your mom is stable but weak. I'd feel better if her blood pressure came up a few notches." I knew what he was saying about Mom. She seems so frail lying there. Her health was never particularly vigorous, and she used to say, "Oh, I'll be fine. I've just got a touch of the croup." Her sister is here now and sitting by her bedside. She'll pull through. I have to believe that.

(Several times Dad has been through the letters since I brought them to the hospital. He got to eat lunch in Mom's room when they took her out of intensive care, and he started reading them to her. Despite the tubes and monitoring machine, she responded. Her eyes actually sparkled, and she smiled when he read his closing paragraph about optimism. Except for the white hair and wrinkles, they looked like two kids on a date as they touched and whispered and kissed each other gently through their cuts and bruises.)

SANCTUARY

The six-year-olds awaiting front teeth, angels all,

    lions and lambs all, lift their wee chins and clear
    eyes to sing

    "Jesus Loves Me" to the Gothic beams and lanyard

    lights hanging chained into the expectant air.

Torch-shaped sconces assist the weak December light to

    illume the color-saturated windows that glorify
    ancient stories

    and challenge our eyes with their radiance.

Candles flame and flicker among the wreathed and
twisted greenery,

    and blood-red pointed leaves aim toward
    sculpted trees,

intensely lighted and shaped like tall pyramids, isosceles

forms that stood in the parched sands so long ago when

the story began.

Then the gathered people—lions and lambs all—sing the familiar

songs: "It Came Upon a Midnight Clear," "Joy to the World,"

"Away in a Manger" and their adequate voices fill the warm

sanctuary with a swelling harmony of belief. And, above all,

hope.

Choose your own canon, but Christmas will come again. Angels we

will hear on high, and the night will be silent.

SAUSAGES

Twilight—
    the day closing, a
    black dome arriving to display
    shards of starlight squinting through
    purplepink above the mountain lake of an
    unfamiliar place.
    My train pierces the soft jelly of the coming night.

Not all—
    who rove are lost. Stillness eludes us. The galaxy spins.
    Blood pumps. Restless souls seek balance by
    moving, moving.
    Alien land or cityscapes ban boredom. By
    donkey cart or jet plane
    the more foreign the place the better. People
    there do not remind me
                   of me.

Brainlocked—
    staring through the darkening window at the

passing scene, I

see the water of the calm lake and the people
strolling peacefully.

I envy them and fantasize: That olive-skinned
man there, the one

with the scar on his cheek, if I were born him
would I have hair on

my back?

Two hours—

from now, in a lusty Bierstube, the lusty woman
will turn to me

and say, "My name is Jasmine. I am vapor." She
will lift her

chicken-voodoo hand and point a pointy finger
at me and declare that

not all who tipple are thirsty.

The lake—

appears empty. Hold on. There is something. A
man in a red boat

with his dog is fishing and an emotion spills
through me too deep

for tears. I become the fisherman. I speak from
my throat and

eat sausages and sing with my wife in choirs.

Never again—

will I have to stare at pages of *meaningful
numbers* in my cubicle cell

two hundred feet above

the gritty street.

DARK MATTERS

You may as well know the truth from the start, I can't write a lick. Couldn't write my way out of a wet paper poke. I'm sitting here at my kitchen table in Missouri talking to a small microphone clipped to my shirt. A cassette tape is recording me, and it's all my daughter's doing. She wants to get down on paper some of our family history and she asked if I would write what she called a memoir. So when I told her I was no good at writing and didn't want to spend a lot of time trying (I believe I actually said not just *no*, but *hell no*), she came right back with this tape-recorder idea and said surely I could do some talking and that I was a good talker and she would get it all typed up. She had me cornered. I do have a good memory, but I ramble on a little too much, so I made her promise me two things. One, since she's a good writer with a college degree, I asked her to be a good editor and clean up my ramblings so they made sense. And, two, she had to agree not to show any of this to anyone in the family or anyone else until after I was dead and gone. That way I'd feel uninhibited to record whatever comes to mind, whether it's good times or bad. The fact that you're reading this, Sherlock, must mean I'm dead.

My name is Buck Walters. I'm seventy-four years old as this tape begins, born in 1920, so obviously it's 1994. There've been some interesting things happen in seventy-four years for sure, so maybe it will be pleasant to reminisce. My folks named me Walter at birth, thinking Walter Walters would be cute. As you can imagine, they were wrong. By age three I didn't care for it. It was in kindergarten at age five that I showed my classmates the dollar bill I had saved up and folded in my pocket, quite a bit of money in those days. So from then on I was Buck. Thank goodness. By second grade very few people could tell you my real name. If they asked I'd lie and tell them, "Jarrett, but call me Buck." If Walter got around I'd never hear the end of it.

I should say right here early on that I was seldom one to question the meaning of life or have my head in the stars or worry too much about death, but I did think of myself as a little moody, or brooding, when I was a young man. Maybe a little bit of a seeker, given to reading books. For one thing, I thought the girls liked that type better— and for another thing, I did feel sorry for myself because we were dirt poor and I was actually, truly, born in a two-room log cabin with an uneven floor, a fireplace for heat and thin clay mortar between the logs that let in a steady Oklahoma breeze. There's a Walmart Supercenter on that spot today. As a young adult my very blood whispered to me that selfish, moody thinking was going to get me nowhere. I quit with the moping, if that's what it was, and went to work. I worked hard—really long, hard hours—to do what needed to be done. Whether it was manual labor, of which there was plenty, or bookkeeping or thinking up a plan for the next day's work, I got it done. When I got to that point, which was right after the war, I quickly began to get ahead.

Please don't get me wrong. I'm not saying I completely lost what is usually called an "inner life"; I didn't. But thinking about what might be or ought to be took a back seat to the day-to-day reality of earning a living. You might think that sounds like drudgery, but for me it was liberating. I began to feel like an independent man, relying on myself and doing some good. I understand that sitting behind a desk or, as in my case, driving a pickup from small town to small town peddling bananas and tomatoes would be numbing to some people. I began to earn a good living, and I liked it. Eventually I got into petroleum distribution and then banking. I think all of us should get over ourselves and get on with it. Make some friends. Live hour to hour, day to day, and see what comes next. There's a great pleasure in that. You can accomplish a lot with family, children, friends, and houses—and most likely that will be your biggest contribution unless you're a genius scientist curing cancer or a brilliant computer whiz inventing robots that will cook and clean and, especially, iron. I can say the results of my down-to-earth approach were pleasing and long lasting. Those close to me appreciated my work ethic. And in the meantime, with my nose to the grindstone and some luck, I became a rich man.

[Daughter's interjection: Dad sells himself too modestly. His words have only been edited and punctuated. When he gets into it and forgets he's being recorded, his thoughts and stories are well spoken and from the heart.]

* * *

I guess I'll just toss in little memories when they pop into my mind and let my daughter put things in order if she wants to. For some reason I just remembered an Indian in my little Oklahoma hometown. He was a guy by the name of Onacona, which means *White Owl*. There were hundreds of Indians in my hometown, and we called all Indian men "Chief" and all Indian women "Squaw," though we hardly ever spoke to the women. That sounds bad now, but back then they didn't mind at all and nothing demeaning was thought about it. They might not mind even today, for all I know. To understand this story you have to know that the Indians of my youth almost never got their pronouns right. They'd call a male "she" and a female "him." Maybe it had something to do with their native Cherokee language. Anyway, White Owl is riding a nice roan horse right down Main Street, when I happened by. His squaw was walking quickly behind. "Hey, Chief," I grinned and called to him. "Why are you riding and making her walk?" He thought for a moment and then quite seriously said, "Him no got horse." A straight answer. I came to appreciate people who offer a straight answer and don't try to shade things a certain way.

Mother and Father weren't churchy people even though they had plenty of respect for religion. They just had to work so hard to make a living they didn't have much time to be churchgoers. I didn't darken many church doors myself until the past couple of years, and now I've been going every Sunday. I started just to please my wife, Mary, but some of it is sinking in now that I'm older. I hope there's something to it all.

Speaking of my dad, I need to talk about him right off the bat. His full name was Jefferson Columbus Walters, and he was the marshal of our little town. But his authority was county wide, and he took the job seriously. He pinned on the six-pointed badge of his office every day and had a droopy, crescent-moon moustache. He'd lost an eye when he was sixteen thanks to a kick in the head from a frisky mare. He wore an eye patch until he was thirty-one and then bought a cheap glass eye. It was pretty obvious. I never saw him in his eye patch because he was fifty-two when I came along from his third wife, who was twenty-seven. His first wife died young, probably of cancer. His second wife was a full-blood Cherokee, so my three older half brothers were half-breeds. Two of them were in the horse business and eventually they joined forces, buying and selling horses and making a good living doing it. They both had a thirst for the firewater. Dad's

Indian wife died young too, why I don't know, so after a while he married my mom, Luna. Family lore claimed she was a quarter Cherokee herself. She wasn't on the Indian rolls of Oklahoma, however, so she didn't get a check from the government, and I don't know to this day whether I'm an eighth or not. There are a lot of stories like that in Oklahoma.

My father was a small man but a proud man. He stood up straight. In fact, he stood so straight he almost reared back, and the thing that impressed me was he didn't seem to have any fear of anything or anybody. He was famous for a while when a known murderer was seen riding horseback through our town coming up from Texas and headed for Arkansas. Dad formed a horseback posse of six men and gave chase. They caught up with him early the next morning at his campsite and he jumped up as they approached and pulled his rifle. Dad was still on horseback when he shot him through the heart and killed him instantly. A Texas Ranger came to our town and claimed the body and took him away. The story was in all the local and regional newspapers. Dad said he was just doing his job, what he got paid for. I remember him as a clean man, who wore clean overalls or dungarees every day. He shaved clean as a whistle every morning.

I knew this Indian boy named Grover, or at least that's what we called him. I'm pretty sure his Cherokee name was *Waya*, meaning *Wolf*. He was opposed to continuing to be something that was not part of mainstream America. He was the only one who thought that way, at least the only one I ever knew about. Every other Indian I knew even a little bit wanted to protect his culture, his heritage, his way of living. But Grover believed all that was finished and he should adapt, understand, and move on to the new world. He became a tenured professor of history at the University of Oklahoma in Norman. I saw him one time at an OU football game against Texas and we had a fifteen-minute talk about our upbringing in a small Oklahoma town and what it meant for him to break away from his traditions. He said he was still close to his aged mother and father, but there'd always been tension about how he'd gone into the white man's world. Even though he'd succeeded. His wife taught math and was named Ruth, a white Anglo woman. They had two kids.

My dad and mother's life together was always overshadowed by money troubles, which no doubt had a great effect on me as an adult. My mother was twenty-five years younger than my dad and I remember hearing big arguments between them about her being seen around other men. Those were sad times for me, dark matters, because I was under ten years old and didn't really understand. I knew things weren't right and it was scary to me thinking they were breaking up and there was no telling what would happen to me or where I'd go. Somehow they stayed together until Dad died at age seventy-two when I was about to turn twenty.

Mother had borne a son out of wedlock before she got together with Dad. Her son was never welcome around our series of tiny rental houses if the marshal was home.

Clyde made a pretty good living as a rodeo clown for several years, moving with the rodeos around Oklahoma and Texas, but I think he finally got tired of broken bones from being butted by Brahman bulls. He partnered up with my two half brothers in their horse business. He didn't mind the firewater either, so the three of them and their wives (all of whom had significant Indian blood) had interesting lives and lots of party time. They were all at least ten or fifteen years older than me, maybe more, so they've all been gone for quite a while. But I liked being around them for their playful attitude.

My third half brother, the oldest, was William Jefferson, always known as Will, and he was cut from different cloth than the other two. He served as a doughboy in World War I and sometimes would walk around in his soldier coat and hat. He was kind of wild. By that I mean that trouble always seemed to find him even though he wasn't looking for it. By all accounts he was pleasant to be around. He got into a lot of fights, but he was never the one who started it. He just didn't walk away or try to avoid a scrap. His Indian wife's English name was Bertha, and they had six children, all boys. The boys idolized their dad. The best story I remember about Will was when a guy by the name of Steen—who had knifed another guy right in the heart and the guy ran about a block and keeled over dead—was being loud and obnoxious in a local bar and restaurant. This was after he killed that guy and was awaiting trial. He'd been drinking and was acting mean and threatening and nobody there could do anything with

him. They called Will. When Will walked in and told
Steen they were leaving, Steen said to back off or he'd kill
him just like he killed the other guy. Will kept walking
right toward Steen and grabbed him by the collar and
yanked him off his barstool and took him out the door
and walked him home. Walked him home and got him
off the streets. Will must have taken after Dad, because he
wasn't afraid of anything or anybody.

I did have a full sister, also older than me, and Avo
was quite a character. Our younger sister Ruth only lived
about six months and died of what they called "summer
complaint." I think that's actually dysentery. Avo told me,
and only me, that she was afraid she killed our little sister.
She was milking a cow we had and carelessly let the cow
kick the half-full bucket over on the filthy barn floor. She
was afraid to tell Mom and Dad. The baby got some of the
milk. It should have been thrown out because of what's
now known as *E. coli*.

Avo was an all-state basketball player for our high
school in the 1930s, even though she wasn't tall. Our girls'
team won the state championship and then played in a
national tournament of some kind and won that. People
will be surprised to learn that girls' basketball was common
back then, but stopped for about two or three decades and
then came back. The women today are better than ever
but they do use a smaller ball than men and the goal is the
same size. Makes shooting a lot easier.

I remember our milk cow we called Miss Stubby
because when I was a boy, clear up to high school, I had to

milk her most every early morning before school. She had a two-foot stub for a tail because the rest of it had been torn off by a dog chasing her and there wasn't enough of it for me to hold on to while I milked. I could count on her to club me with that stub about a dozen times while I tried to milk her. You'd think she'd be glad to be milked so she could graze and chew her cud all day, but I always thought she had it in for me. She would give around two gallons and that was a big part of our food supply. We had the best butter and cream and gravy from that old cow, and when I think about it I can still taste it. Beans and biscuits with cream gravy and sugar syrup, nothing's better. Now we think things like that aren't good for you because anything that tastes good must be bad for you. Sad.

Halloween was always prank time when I was a kid. Some of it bordered on vandalism. The one that stands out in my mind is when I was about thirteen or fourteen and a bunch of us boys, including several older ones, were roaming the streets like a pack of wolves when somebody remembered seeing a dead horse in a field outside of town. Another guy remembered a wagon we could get and we took that wagon and turned it over on the dead horse, then got a hold of the horse's feet and neck and rolled it up on the wagon and lifted the whole thing up and hauled the wagon to the middle of town and dumped that horse carcass right on Main Street. There were no streetlights so it was total darkness, but we knew there'd be a fuss the next day. That was bad enough, but the real story was Elroy Simpson, one of the older boys. He kept being sick to his stomach from the smell while we were moving the horse so he decided he needed to stick his finger down his throat to gag and vomit. He did that. He was sick all night. The next morning he saw that the very finger he'd stuck down his throat had dead-horse meat under the fingernail. Then he was even sicker. He was about as sick as any human being could be for three days, throwing up and missing school, so I guess that year the joke was on us. Now that we're oldsters, we are once in a while subject to vandalism on Halloween that makes me think I'm being punished for my young teen escapades. There've been several incidents of Mary's little statues being stolen from our yard. For example, we're missing a frog and fountain that had to weigh at least seventy pounds and a little boy and girl out in the flower bed by the road that had to weigh a hundred.

I didn't mention on the earlier tapes the violent things I saw growing up. I wasn't even a teenager yet when there was a house on fire and a bunch of us ran to see it. It was the house of an old, retired doctor who was known to be a drinker and maybe even a dope addict. Yes, we knew about those things even back then. The fire had killed him, and we were standing near the front door of what was left of that house when they brought out his body. He was literally burned to a charcoal; there wasn't much left of him. That left a very vivid impression on me. Another time I was walking down the road to go swimming in Honey Creek, about two miles from town, and a stave truck came down the road so I stuck out my thumb to ask for a ride. There were two guys inside the truck and one standing up in the rear flatbed not hanging on to anything. The driver swerved at me to scare me, then swerved back. The guy in the back lost his balance and fell out right under the dual wheels, which ran over him and killed him on the spot. He was a young guy, maybe eighteen years old. It scared me so bad I was in shock for several days. I couldn't eat. The only place I wanted to be was home with my momma. That also left a very vivid impression on me to this day. I've never forgotten, and I've even had dreams about it.

I'm sure many people have had the same experience as I did with jobs back in those days, and I'm talking about the 1930s mostly. I had a shoeshine stand, a newspaper route, and worked for the Graham brothers in their grocery store. I worked there on weekends, Fridays and Saturdays. Some of those Saturdays were rough after getting tackled and bruised in our Friday-night football games when I was the team quarterback. Sore or not, I still had to carry hundred-pound sacks of animal feed and be on my feet all day. We candled eggs and stocked shelves and all of that too. The pay was twenty cents an hour. I got two dollars for a ten-hour day. Come Saturday night we'd chip in for gas, a nickel or a dime each, maybe a quarter if you were feeling flush, and buy gas for whoever had managed to get a car from their folks. We had enough left over for the movie, which I think I remember was twenty cents. Then after the show we'd eat hamburgers and chili at the local café. I can still taste the chili, just like the biscuits and cream gravy; it was wonderful. Saturday night was something to look forward to.

High school flew by with our football team almost never losing a game. I think we only lost one game in my three years as varsity quarterback. We played an Indian school one year, and I got my bell rung real good. A big Indian kid hit me so hard on an end-around play that I could see stars. No doubt in my mind it was a concussion, but in those days nobody knew much about that. I stayed in the game. After I called the same play three times in a row, our coach called time out and we huddled and he asked me what I was doing? I found out later I just stared at him and didn't answer so he figured out I was dinged and took me out. After about five minutes I was OK again. I told him so and went back into the game. We won.

I applied to our nearby junior college and got a full football scholarship, meaning I could go to college for free. Best deal I'd ever been offered. Our football team was really good, probably the second best in Oklahoma after OU. I didn't study much but was getting by fine until, and I'm not proud of it, there was a glitch.

We always had card games and sometimes dice games in the dorm for pennies and nickels, which was very much against the rules. I was good at that, especially at poker, and could count on a little extra spending money from gambling. But one evening somebody turned us in. I wish I knew who it was so I could go knock his teeth out, although at my age that's not likely. Besides, he'd be as old as me so he might just take his teeth out instead of me knocking them out. The card game was in my room. When the housemother came and rapped sharply on the door, everybody except me went out the second-story window and got away. I was called before the dorm committee or citizenship committee or whatever you want to call it and was kicked out of school. That ended my college career and my transcript reads "incomplete." Today I realize it really didn't matter. Our football coach tried to go to bat for me and get temporary probation or something like that, but there were two old spinster women who wouldn't have it any other way. That had to be 1940, and I have them to thank for getting me on the track that worked out for me—hard work, a little luck, and marriage to Mary.

We met thanks to a mutual friend during my first year in college. This guy on the team said, "You've got to see this gal." So we went down to the Princess Theater where Mary worked the popcorn stand. I was struck from the beginning. We dated a little bit, and then when I was kicked out of college and started working various jobs full time, we dated a lot. Somehow we talked about "what ifs" and getting married was one of those. So we went with four friends over to the local judge's house and he married us on the spot. It was August of 1941. He charged two dollars, which I hated to part with. The judge said, "Well, I hope you don't come back." It's fifty-three years later, and we haven't been back. It hasn't always been roses—and once, only once, I got so angry and frustrated I slapped and pushed her and immediately regretted it. But by now we have such a history together and have built such a good life and our three kids have turned out well that we won't be going back. We comfort each other as old age catches up to us and it gets harder to go up and down stairs.

Talking about Mary reminds me to say something about her dad. Riley was a tough old bird, a curly-haired Irishman who was a left-handed butcher. He ended up owning the grocery store where he worked, changed its name to Pennysaver Market, and before long had opened two others in nearby towns. Might have been one of the first grocery-store chains. He was doing great until the Depression hit, and he lost it all. Paid every bill he owed and walked away without a dime. It wasn't long until he opened another Pennysaver in our hometown. He lived upstairs. Things had gotten a little better, and he was the only employee so the only overhead was a little rent and utilities. He didn't believe in insurance. He opened at 7 a.m. and closed at 9 p.m. every day of the year, every minute of it by himself. I remember him saying, "If your income doesn't match your outflow, then your upkeep will be your downfall." Cute. Anyway, one night he was walking up the dark stairs to go to bed and a robber who knew he had the day's proceeds on him was waiting. The guy hit Riley in the head with something, maybe a billy club or a bat, but Riley didn't go down and fought back with his cash bag. He hit the robber in the neck with the heavy bag and the guy took off running while pennies, nickels, dimes and a few quarters went tumbling down the stairs. A little clean up and Riley was off to bed. Didn't even call the police until the next morning. Another time was more serious. Two guys came in at closing time with a gun. They moved him away from the cash register and started cleaning it out. Riley jumped the one with the gun, but it went off and shot him in the gut. The armed robbers got away. He staggered out into the empty street, bleeding like crazy, and started walking to the police station. He was reeling side to side when a car came by and the driver got him to the hospital. The bullet had missed any vital organs and was stuck under the skin on his left back. He was back on his feet in two days and running the store. He gave the police a perfect description, and the two armed robbers were caught a week later and spent years in prison. Tough old bird.

Of course Pearl Harbor happened four months after Mary and I got married. What was expected of me? Some of my friends enlisted immediately and were eager to kill Japs and Germans. I was kind of on hold. I knew I'd be drafted and go to war, but I can't really say I was eager since Mary had gotten pregnant immediately after we married. She had a little girl who died of spina bifida after a few months, I can't remember exactly how many months but no more than six or eight, and her short life was misery for all of us, especially her. I'm pretty sure they know how to do surgery for spina bifida now and fix it. Not then. My draft notice came while she was still alive so I was gone to US Army basic training in Texas when she died. After basic, I had a week's leave so I went back to Oklahoma.

Unknown to us at the time, I got Mary pregnant again during that week and nine months later things got complicated. I was assigned to a riflemen's company after basic and we were being further trained on Thompson submachine guns, mortars, grenade launchers, and flamethrowers at another base in Alabama when a telegram came that Mary was about to give birth again. It was September of 1943, and we were expected to ship out to England any time. I explained to my company commander that we'd already lost a baby and I needed a ten-day pass to try and be there for the birth of our second. He said no. Something inside me went haywire and I called that captain a son of a bitch and either he was going to sign for my pass or I was going AWOL and they could throw me in jail when I got back or whatever they wanted to do but I was going to be in Oklahoma day after tomorrow. My face was red and felt hot after I said that. I knew he could throw me into the stockade if I left the base and he wanted to. This was a moment I look back on now and can only imagine how my life might have turned out differently and ended a lot sooner. I'll never forget him and can close my eyes today and see him lean back in his chair. He was a guy by the name of Bowers, Captain Bowers. "I shouldn't do this, Walters," was exactly what he said, "but I'm going to sign it for you. When you get back you remember to be the best PFC in the whole damn army." "Yes, sir," I said, and shook his hand and walked out of his office with my pass.

Two days later, after a lot of hitchhiking—which was normal in those days, but I'd hate to try it now—I was there for the birth of a perfectly healthy son. A week after that I was showing my pass to the MPs at the gate of Fort McClellan, Alabama, and they were telling me that my rifle company had shipped out forty-eight hours earlier. I was reassigned to the Joliet Army Ammunitions Plant in Illinois and spent the next year and a half moving up to being a sergeant first class supervisor in that plant making all kinds of explosives. I never went to war. My rifle company was in the second wave at D-Day on the beaches of Normandy, and out of a hundred twenty or so men, only five survived the war. My baby son's birth and Captain Bowers saved my life. I've had guilty feelings about that. I was just as patriotic as anyone.

I've already talked about after the war and peddling bananas, gasoline, and money as a banker, and about my work ethic eventually making me a wealthy man with a lot to be thankful for, but I have to admit my tolerance for making tape recordings is beginning to fade. My daughter has agreed that I should take a break. [Tape ends.]

[Mary's interjection: Our daughter asked me to do the same thing Buck has done, tell my life story to a tape recorder and answer the long list of questions she's created. She has also improved on my meanderings, as she did on her dad's, and typed it all up and put it into a binder. My life is less interesting than Buck's, in many ways, but I was there to share it all. It's been quite a journey.]

[Daughter's second interjection: Dad took a break all right, a ten-year break during which he and my mom had some of the best years of their lives. They became good at road travel, mostly in nice motor homes. Dad loved to drive and they would stay in those fancy motor-home parks in Texas and Florida in the winter. They had a beautiful house in a gated subdivision and my two brothers and I visited often. They even learned how to have friends and throw a party once in a while.]

[Daughter's third interjection: He was just starting to record a little bit again when it happened. He was eighty-four, almost eighty-five. I was actually there and brought takeout for supper. I ended up witnessing what we would later learn was a massive stroke that killed him. We'd been sitting at the kitchen table when he fell backward and the ambulance took him away with the microphone still clipped to his shirt and the cassette recorder stuck in his pants pocket. I didn't realize it was still recording and certainly didn't realize he was dying. He had the freakish experience of recording his own death. His voice was weak. There were long pauses between words. I didn't think I could understand what he was saying, but after listening maybe twenty times I got it. I present it now, translated accurately, I hope, with eerie sounds at the end I will never understand.]

I'm in an ambulance. Bed with wheels. I think I fell. My voice doesn't sound like me. (*He groans.*) My head is gravel. Hurts. (*Another groan.*) The ambulance has siren on. Sound makes head hurt worse (*Groan.*) (*Shallow breathing.*) (*Twenty second pause.*) I need to be calm. Am I dying? It doesn't seem that bad. They stopped. They're taking me into a hospital. They're taking me down a long hallway. My head is mush and hurts worse now. Light then not light. Lights are strong from hallway ceiling then darker in between. When light gets strong then it gets dark again. Bright lights overhead remind me summer days that made me squint. When light is strong I see high school friends. Dark again . . . Now I see a different light. I see them all, my old friends. Mary? Mary? I'm done. (*Long groan and shallow rattle.*)

[Daughter's fourth interjection: You may have trouble with this, but there is another minute of sound on the tape, with static and ER hubbub and something else that's hard to make sense of. I retrieved the microphone and recorder just as they were loading him from the gurney onto an operating table to take him in. He did not awaken. It sounds like a party with laughing people and clinking glasses, or is that wishful thinking? Deep human voices sounding as if underwater or in slow motion are saying something that I desperately want to be "Welcome." I miss him terribly.]

AFTERWORD

This book is a work of fiction. Names, characters, places, and incidents either are products of my imagination or are used fictitiously. Any resemblance to actual events or locales or persons, living or dead, is entirely coincidental.

The occasional element may be inspired by real events. For example, the story "Dark Matters" is effectuated by the fact that my sister Patty did, indeed, coax our parents into telling their stories into a tape recorder. Therefore some of the experiences described in the story have a factual basis, according to our father's descriptions. Others, not so much.

The fake-news Christmas letters were originally written and sent out to friends as a joke, just for the fun of it. Each one escalates toward its conclusion so no one would mistake it for truth. However, one particularly fleeceable (or should we say trusting) friend, *completely believed* the first letter clear to the end. When he showed it to his wife in amazement she quickly steered him straight. I remind him of that incident as often as possible.